First time author Sarah Prineas is already hard at work writing the next book of *The Magic Thief* trilogy. She lives in Iowa City, Iowa, with her husband John and their children Maud and Theo.

You can visit her online at:
www.sarah-prineas.com
or on *The Magic Thief* website:
www.magicthief.co.uk

Praise for *The Magic Thief*:

'I couldn't put it down. Wonderful, exciting stuff.' – Diana Wynne Jones author of *Howl's Moving Castle*

'Sarah Prineas's vivid descriptions made me feel as if I was walking right next Conn, her young resourceful hero.' – D. J. MacHale author of the Penndragon series

'Spellbinding . . . a joy to peruse. It is beautifully illustrated, interspersed with extracts from Nevery's journal, and contains appendices, and maps. The website is worth visiting too, for its illustration of Device and joy, confirmation that the future novels will contain dragons! A wonderful book, which I recommend unreservedly.' – *Bookbag*

'Thief-erific!
Magic-tastic!
Biscuit-tacular!' Ysabeau S. Wilce author of *Flora Segunda*

THE MAGIC THIEF

BOOK ONE

SARAH PRINEAS

ILLUSTRATIONS BY
ANTONIO JAVIER CAPARO

Quercus

First published in Great Britain in 2008
This paperback edition published in 2009 by

Quercus
21 Bloomsbury Square
London
WC1A 2NS

Published in America by HarperCollins Children's Books
a division of HarperCollins Publishers, Inc.
1350 Avenue of the Americas, New York 10019, USA

ISBN 978 1 84724 699 8

10 9 8 7 6 5 4

This book printed and bound in England by
Clays Ltd, St Ives plc.

TO MAUD,
WHO LAUGHED IN ALL
THE RIGHT PLACES

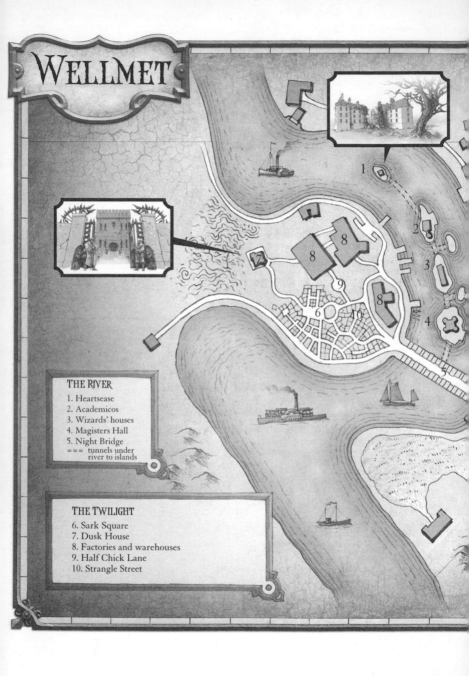

WELLMET

THE RIVER

1. Heartsease
2. Academicos
3. Wizards' houses
4. Magisters Hall
5. Night Bridge
=== tunnels under
   river to islands

THE TWILIGHT

6. Sark Square
7. Dusk House
8. Factories and warehouses
9. Half Chick Lane
10. Strangle Street

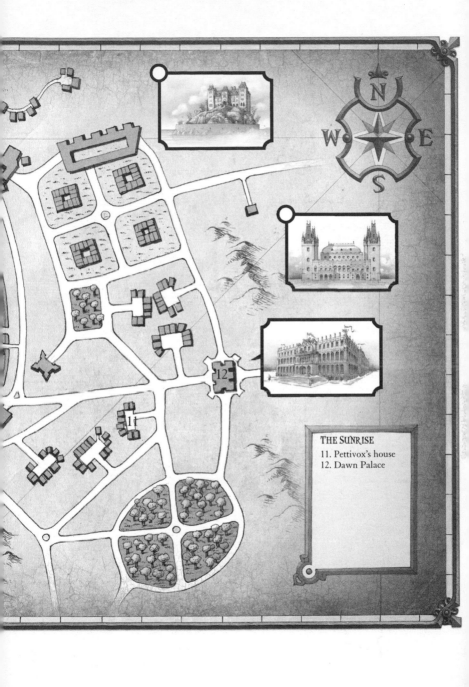

THE SUNRISE

11. Pettivox's house
12. Dawn Palace

CHAPTER 1

A thief is a lot like a wizard. I have quick hands. And I can make things disappear. But then I stole the wizard's locus magicalicus and nearly disappeared myself forever.

It was a late night in the Twilight, black-dark as the inside of a burglar's bag. The streets were deserted. A sooty fog crept up from the river, and the alleyways echoed with shadows. Around me I felt the city, echoing and empty, desolate and dead.

The cobblestones under my bare feet were slick with the evening's rain. No luck that day for my quick, pick-pocket hands, and I hadn't managed to filch my supper or a bit of copper to buy it with. I was hollow with hunger. I might have tried somewhere else, except that the Underlord had a word out on me, and his minions would beat the fluff out of me if they could. Keeping an eye out, I lurked in an alleyway.

Now it was late. The rain started up again, not a hard rain, but a cold one, just enough to get into your bones and make you shiver. A good night for misery eels. I hunched into my lurking spot and thought about warm dinners.

Then I heard it. Step step *tap*. Step step *tap*. I edged back into my alley shadows to wait, and along he came. Old man, I thought. A bent, bearded, cloak-wearing old croakety croak leaning on a cane. Climbing the steep street toward me. Muttering to himself. His purse, I decided, would be paying for my dinner, though he didn't know it yet.

I was a shadow, a breath of air, light-feather fingers and – *quick hands* – I ghosted up behind him, dipped into his cloak pocket, grabbed what I found within, and was gone. Away clean.

Or so I thought. The old man went on, not noticing a thing, and I slipped back into my alley and opened my hand to see what I'd got for my trouble.

Even in the shadows, the thing I'd stolen was darker than dark, and though it was small, a stone no bigger than a baby's fist, it was heavier than the heart of a man on his way to the gallows tree. It was a magical thing. The wizard's locus magicalicus. As I stared down at the wizardly stone, it started to glow. Soft at first, with the red warmth of coals in a winter hearth. Then, a sudden fierce flash of lightning and the alley was alive with dancing, flashing light, the shadows fleeing like frightened black cats.

I heard the wizard coming back. Step step *tap*. Step step *tap*. Quickly I fisted the stone and shoved it down deep into my pocket. Darkness fell again. As I turned, blinking the brights from my eyes to look, the old man came tip-tapping around my corner, and, reaching out with a big hand, grabbed me by the shoulder.

'Well, boy,' he said. His voice was strong and gravelly.

I stood still. I know trouble when it grabs me.

The old man looked down at me with keen-glancing eyes. Silence for a long, dark moment. In my pocket, the stone weighed and warmed. Then he said, 'You look hungry.'

Well, yes. I was. Carefully, cautiously, I nodded.

'Then I will buy you some dinner,' the old man said. 'Roast pork, perhaps? Potatoes and pie?'

I swallowed. My head was telling me this was not a good idea. The old man was a wizard, clear as clear, and what kind of fool sits down to eat dinner with a wizard?

But my empty-since-yesterday stomach was telling me even louder that it wanted pork and peppered potatoes and pie. It told me to nod and I did.

'Well then,' the old man wizard said. 'The

chophouse on the corner is still open.' He let me go and started step-tapping down the street, and I went with him. 'I am Nevery,' he said. 'And your name?'

Telling wizards your name is generally not a good idea. I didn't answer. Just walked along beside him. The wizard seemed to be looking ahead to the chophouse on the corner, but I caught a glimpse of his keen-gleam eyes, watching me from under the brim of his hat.

The chophouse was lit by a coal fire in the hearth and was empty except for its keeper. 'Dinner,' the wizard ordered, and held up two fingers. The chophouse keeper nodded and went to fetch the food. We settled at a table, me with my back against the wall, Nevery blocking my way to the door.

'Well, boy,' the wizard said, taking off his hat. In the brighter light I saw that his eyes were black and his hair, beard, and eyebrows silver grey. Beneath his dark grey cloak, he wore black trousers and a black frock coat with a velvet collar and an embroidered black waistcoat, all of it just a bit shabby, as if he'd once had more money than he did now. He leaned his gold-knobbed cane against the table. 'A cold, wet night for travellers, is it not?'

A cold, wet night for anyone, I thought. I nodded.

He looked at me. I looked back.

'Yet you seem healthy enough,' he said, as if talking to himself. 'No ill effects that I can see.'

Ill effects? What was he talking about?

'You never did tell me your name,' he said.

And I wasn't going to, either. I shrugged.

Nevery opened his mouth to say something else, when the chophouse keeper delivered our food, plunking down full plates before us.

The pork chops were fragrant and crisp, the potatoes swimming in butter with a sprinkling of black pepper over their shiny brown backs. The chophouse keeper returned briefly and added a plate of pie oozing with berries and dusted with sugar. The wizard said something, but I didn't hear him. I picked up my fork and cut open a potato. I let the butter soak in for a second and then took an enormous bite.

'I said,' the wizard said, staring at me, 'that

my locus magicalicus will likely kill you, boy, very soon. I'm astonished it hasn't done so already.'

I gulped. My bite of potato slid like a lump of lead down my throat and I heard the echo as it dropped into my empty stomach.

Kill me, did he say? The locus stone would kill me? I slid my hand into my pocket. And then I watched myself pull out the stone. It lay in my palm like a soft-edged bit of night.

I blinked, and the stone swelled, and a heavy, night-dark mass filled my hands. The firelight flickered out.

In the distance, I heard the chophouse keeper scream. The wizard snatched up his knobbed cane and leaped to his feet.

In my hands, the stone's warmth turned to ice. It grew larger, and though I tried to put it down, it wouldn't let me go. The freezing heaviness grew and expanded until it was all around me, dragging me down into a seething black pit where the wind stabbed me with needles of ice and roared with a voice that rumbled in my bones.

I peered up through the lashing darkness.

The wizard Nevery loom-doomed up before me.

'Tell me your name!' he shouted.

I shook my head. The wind shrieked and tore with icy fingers at my hair and clothes.

Nevery shouted again; I could barely hear his voice above the wind. 'If you don't tell me your name, fool, I cannot save you!'

The wind whipped around me. Cold air flowed from the stone, reaching out with icy fingers, pulling me in, and I pushed it away and shouted my name, 'Connwaer!'

In the distance, I heard Nevery's strong, gravelly voice shout my name along with other words, a magical spell. Then I felt his hand, warm, solid, close over mine and take the stone.

The wind died. The air warmed. All was quiet.

After a while, I opened my eyes to find myself lying on the wooden floor of the chophouse, the fire flickering in the fireplace and Nevery at the table taking a last bite of berry pie. He wiped his mouth on a napkin and leaned back in his chair, looking down at me.

The stone was nowhere to be seen.

'Well then, boy,' he said, his eyes gleaming. 'My locus magicalicus ought to have killed you the moment you laid your thieving fingers on it. But it did not. And because you are not dead, you interest me.'

I blinked and climbed shakily to my feet. On the table, my plate of pork chops and potatoes waited for me. And the berry pie dusted with sugar. I could have made a run for it, then. He couldn't have caught me. Quick-dart for the door and back out into the steep, rain-dark streets of Wellmet. But I didn't. Because I interested the wizard.

The thing is, I make a good thief, me and my quick hands. But I'll make an even better wizard's apprentice.

Arrived back in this accursed city after nightfall. Dratted city guards tried to arrest me. Prison if I'm caught here. Used remirrimer spell, eluded them. Forced to retreat to Twilight, west of river.

Dangerous place.

Banishment from Wellmet a long misery, travel from city to city, my grimoire lost, my magic weakened. Would not have come back but for letter from Brumbee.

My dear Nevery,

I know that when you left you swore never to return to Wellmet, but dire events are taking place in the city. We have been monitoring the magical levels and have made an alarming discovery. The level of magic in Wellmet is ebbing. This has been going on for years, but lately the level has fallen rather alarmingly and abruptly, and we magisters can discover no reason why this should be so. The duchess is no help, of course. You must return and aid the city in its time of need. Please tell no one that I have written to you.

Really, Nevery, I do not know what to do. You must help.

Very sincerely yours,
Brumbee, Magister,
Master of Wellmet Academicos,
&c.

Letter did not mention fact that I have been banished from Wellmet for past twenty years. Typical of Brumbee. Man's too worried to think about consequences of inviting me back to city.

To do:
1. *Find accommodation in Twilight*
2. *Meet Brumbee*
3. *Meet with Underlord Crowe*
4. *Hire muscle. Benet?*

After arrival in Twilight, went in search of dinner.

Note to self: check locus magicalicus for adosyncratichi, be sure it's unaffected by tonight's adventure.

Was not planning on taking on servant. Will probably not keep him, as most likely not worth trouble. Boy thief is wrapped up in a blanket on the hearth, sound asleep. From here, looks like bundle of rags with dirty bare feet sticking out one end and shock of dirty dark hair out the other.

Only time for short entry tonight. Am weary from the journey and must think on what is to come.

CHAPTER 2

On my first apprentice morning, the wizard Nevery woke me up. He stood all-tall, wearing his grey wizard's robe, and nudged me again with his foot.

'Get up, boy.' He pointed with his cane at a basin of water on the table. 'Wash yourself and join me in the chophouse for breakfast.'

Breakfast!

As he left the room, I rubbed the sleep out of my eyes and rolled myself out of the

blanket.

Wash up, the wizard had said. I went to the table, to the basin of water. Stuck my finger in. Brrr. Cold as cobbles.

I went downstairs for breakfast and found the wizard at the same table we'd shared the night before. Nevery sat with his knob-headed cane propped against the wall beside his chair, drinking tea. His cloak, I noticed, had a patch on the sleeve with a picture of an hourglass with wings on it, stitched in dark blue thread.

'Did you wash?' Nevery asked.

I shrugged, looking past him at the table. There were hot biscuits and bacon and porridge and tea. I started for my seat but stopped when he grabbed me.

'You washed?'

Well, no. Not yet. I shook my head.

He pointed toward the stairs. 'You wash. And then you may eat.'

And if I didn't make it quick, he'd eat all the bacon, no doubt. I ran up the stairs to the room. I stripped off my shirt and splashed up some water and scrubbed my hands and face.

Shivering, I went down again.

Nevery nodded.

I sat down and reached for the biscuits.

The wizard stared at me while I ate. He was looking at me, but he was thinking about something else.

All right with me. I had porridge with butter to deal with. The chophouse keeper brought more things to eat. At last I finished the last crumb of pie left over from the night before.

'Had enough?' Nevery asked.

I nodded.

'I should think so,' he muttered, getting to his feet and taking up his cane. 'Come along, boy.'

He headed for the door, jamming his flat-topped, wide-brimmed hat onto his head and pausing to settle up with the chophouse keeper, then striding out onto the street.

Not one to stand about talking, was he?

'Where we going?' I asked, catching up.

He gave me one of his keen-gleam glances and strode on. I kept up, having to run a few steps now and then to stay with him.

Nevery turned onto Strangle Street, then down Fleetside, glancing at the falling-down houses and dark shops as he passed, looking for something. At last he stopped before a tavern, the kind of smokehole you have to take two steps down to get inside, the kind of place people go to make dark deals.

'Wait here, boy,' Nevery said, and swept-stepped down into the tavern.

I leaned against the brick wall outside. The wind blew down the street, stirring up the rubbish in the gutters, poking cold fingers down the back of my shirt. The cobblestones were like ice under my feet. Out around me, the city felt shivery and empty. I hugged myself to keep warm.

After a while, Nevery came up out of the tavern, followed by a thick-necked, tall man with spiky hair and a face like a bare-knuckles brawl. Muscle, minion, man of the hench. He wore a plain brown suit with a knitted red waistcoat under it and a wide, brass-buckled belt and, from the looks of it, kept a knife and an almost-empty purse string in his coat pocket.

He'd be working for Nevery, I guessed, so I wouldn't try to steal them.

He hulked up the steps, folded his huge arms, and glared down at me. 'This him, sir?' His voice was deep and growling.

Yes, the wizard's apprentice, I opened my mouth to say, but Nevery beat me to it.

'It is,' Nevery said. He paused to thread a few copper lock coins onto his purse string.

'I'm Conn,' I added.

The new muscle leaned down and spoke in a low voice, so Nevery couldn't hear him. 'Stay out of my way, you.' He showed me his fist.

All right, I got the message. I edged away from him.

'Come along,' Nevery said. He went off down the street, swinging his cane, and the hired muscle went with him.

I followed, trying to listen in on their discussion, but they kept their voices low.

We ended up at Dusk House, where one of Wellmet's worst lived. Crowe. Underlord. Are you *sure* you want to go here, Nevery? I wanted to ask. But I kept quiet.

From the outside, Crowe's place wasn't too bad. Big iron gates out the front, high wall with spikes on top. Inside, a tall stone mansion house. Hard place to get into, hard place to get out of. Not someplace I wanted to go back to. But I reckoned being with Nevery would be protection enough.

Nevery had a word with the two minions at the gate, who let us in. Then he had a word with the four minions at the front door, who let us in.

'We'll take you to Underlord Crowe,' one of the minions said. 'But the muscle stays here.'

'Very well.' Nevery sounded calm. But I saw how hard he was gripping his cane. 'Benet, wait here.' He turned to go with the minion, and I started after him. He paused, looked down at me. 'You stay too, boy.'

I watched him go off down the hallway, the cane going *tap tap* on the shiny black floor. At the other end of the hall, he and the minion went through a tall, black door, which slammed behind them.

I looked around. One of the minions had gone with Nevery. Two had gone back to their guardroom by the front door. That left one watching me and Nevery's new muscle man. Benet stood with his feet braced, arms folded, glaring at the minion, who stared back at him.

Keeping my head down, I sat on the cold floor with my back against the wall.

At that, the minion shifted his glare to me. His eyes narrowed. 'Here now. I know you, don't I?'

I sat very still.

The minion nodded. 'You're that lockpick. Crowe has a word out on you.'

Drats.

The minion came over and, with hard hands, gripped me by the shoulders and yanked me to my feet. I shot Benet a glance, but he stood with his arms folded. No help.

'My master will want a word with you,' the minion growled.

A *word* was not what the Underlord wanted from me.

All at the same moment, I kicked out at the minion's shin and twisted my shoulders and I was free. Ducking under his reaching arms, I raced down the shiny stone hallway toward the door Nevery had gone through.

'Here, you!' the minion shouted. Then he called for the other minions and lumbered after me.

I went through the door into an empty hallway. The second door I came to was unlocked, so I darted through and slammed it closed. I was in another hallway.

I needed to find Nevery. My bare feet made no noise as I ran down the hallway, pausing to try each door. Locked, locked, locked. The hallway turned; I crouched down to peer around the corner. If a guard is looking out for intruders, he looks at his eye level, not down near the floor.

In one direction, nothing but empty hallway. Down the other, two minions outside a door. Crowe still used it as his office, I guessed. Nevery was in there. I backed away from the turning and tried the nearest doorknob, a bumpy brass thing with a big keyhole. Locked. I peeked through the keyhole, checking for light: none. Put my ear against the door: silence.

I fished my lockpick wires out of my pocket

and picked the lock, clean. Easing open the door, I slid inside and pushed it shut again. The room was dark, but I could make out another door in the shadows at the other end.

I crossed the room, quick-quiet to the other door, and did the thing with the lockpicks again. Still clear. Went through the next room, to the next door.

Along the bottom of this door was a line of light. I crouched down and peered through the keyhole. Couldn't see much. Flickering werelight, maybe a shelf of books, the corner of a gold-gilt picture frame.

Then a sound. *Click-tick, click tick, click-tick-tick-tick*. I knew what made that sound. The Underlord. A long time ago I'd done something stupid – picked Crowe's pocket to see what he carried around with him. And what had I got for my trouble? The click-ticker. It was a little hand-sized metal device holding four bone discs with notches on them. Crowe used it for counting, for calculating, and each time a number came up, the device went *click-tick*.

From inside the room, Nevery said

something in a deep growl. He sounded angry.

As I turned away from the keyhole, I realized that the room had a third door.

I went over and crouched down to peer through the ornate keyhole. A man was standing directly opposite the door, shouting at someone else. The man was a white-haired wizard, but not Nevery; he wore a black robe with gold trim and had a locus magicalicus hanging from a gold chain around his neck.

'—without the slowsilver!' he shouted. 'I must have another measure of it at least, or—' He lowered his voice and I couldn't hear exactly what he said, but it sounded deadly, like sharp knives in a dark alley. Scowling, he pointed toward the corner of the room and I heard another door open and slam shut. Then the wizard turned his back and went to a bookcase. He looked around, and then pressed a panel beside the top shelf. The bookcase swung open to reveal a dark doorway. The top of a stairway, I realized. The wizard went down. The bookcase-door stayed open.

What was he up to? Wizardly things,

maybe, and as a wizard's apprentice, I should follow him and find out. Quickly I pulled out my wires and got to work on the lock. It was fancy, but it was a good one, with flanges, studs, *and* crenellations. Finally – *calm breath, quick fingers* – I got the wires to click into place and the lock turned over. I eased the door open and peered into the room. Empty.

I crossed the room to the stairway; it gaped like a pit, dark. I went down a few steps and listened, then went farther, down and down, deeper into the darkness. The stairs were narrow and steep, and I kept my hand on the wall to steady myself. At last, I came to a turning. I peered around. Nothing, just the dim outline of another turning ahead, with lights beyond it. I crept down.

When I reached the next turning, I crouched in the darkness on the step and peered around the corner. Quickly, I pulled back. Bright lights, movement, a big space. Too many people down there to go any farther. I heard clanking, the sound of metal hammering on metal, a grinding of gears, a man's voice, cursing. An acrid smell, like burnt metal, hung in the stairway and prickled in my throat.

I listened for a few more moments, then heard steps coming up from below. Holding my breath, I skiffed up the stairs and out the bookcase-door, then across the room and into the dark room beyond. I swung the door closed and used my lockpick wires to lock it again.

Something was going on. Crowe had a workshop or something down there, and who knew what else. He and this white-haired wizard were up to something, clear as clear. I'd have to work it out.

But now it was time to get back to the front door.

Quietly, checking the doors as I went, I skiffed back to the hallway, then back to the entryway.

I slithered through the door. Just Benet-the-Muscle at the other end, no sign of Underlord minions. I cat-footed it back down the black shiny stone hallway.

As I coasted up, Benet reached out with one long arm and grabbed me, then gave me a swat across the face. I'd gotten worse, but I wasn't expecting it, so I went crashing off into the wall, banged the back of my head, and bit my lip.

Benet didn't say anything, just folded his arms again and stared down at me.

My ears were ringing from the blow as Nevery and the minion came through the door at the end of the hallway. *Tap tap tap* went Nevery's cane on the polished stone floor. I was glad to see him. Not everybody walks out of a meeting with the Underlord. Nevery gave me one of his keen-gleam glances as he came up but didn't say anything. The minions with him glared at me, but they didn't say anything, either.

Staying as far from Benet as I could, I followed Nevery as we left Dusk House. From the sound of the wizard's words with Benet, the meeting had not gone well.

I hoped Nevery knew better than to deal with Crowe. Only one thing ever happened to anybody who crossed the Underlord. And it involved weights and chains and the river on a dark night. Made me shiver just thinking about it.

From Nevery Flinglas, Wizard to
Her Grace, Willa Forestal, Duchess of Wellmet.

Your Grace,
Recently, I was made aware that Wellmet
has been suffering from a decline in its level
of magic. I decided to visit the city to see if
this is true. Since my return from exile —
yes, I am here — I have noticed the decay
and desolation that, according to my readings
on the subject, is characteristic of magical
decline. Many houses lie empty and rotting,
the streets are desolate, the people listless;
the very fabric of the city is unravelling. No
doubt, you have magisters working on the
problem. They are incompetent fools, as you
well know.

I am here; I offer my services. If you

will lift the order of exile — if you deem
that twenty years banishment is enough — I
will put all of my energies into identifying
the cause of the magical decline and then act
to correct it.

You may send a response with my man,
Benet, or send a letter to me at the
chophouse on Half-Chick Lane in the
Twilight.

Yours sincerely,

NEVERY

Post Script: Willa, if you choose to again
force me from the city, I will leave and you
may deal with the problem yourself.

From Her Grace, Willa Forestal,
Duchess of Wellmet,
To Nevery Flinglas, Wizard.

Nevery,
I am quite aware of your return. And
I readily admit that Wellmet has a
problem and that the magisters have
done little, or perhaps nothing, to discover
what is wrong. As always, I place the
city's needs above my own, and so I am
lifting the order of exile. However, one
wrong step, Nevery, and I will see
you cast out again. No pyrotechnic
experiments. Do not try my patience.

On this fourth day of Nonembry,
I am
Duchess Willa Forestal, &c.

Duchess has responded to letter; however, must tread carefully, as she could easily change her mind, have me arrested. Letter from duchess means I can move back into Heartsease. House is surely falling to pieces, but best place for my purposes. Tomorrow, first thing: leave chophouse, put servant boy and Benet to work making place habitable.

Once settled there, must discover magisters' position. Likely boy useless as servant. And more trouble than he is worth. His breakfast alone cost four copper locks:

Three biscuits
Bacon
Four eggs
Two cups tea
Cup of milk
Bowl of porridge with:
    Butter
    Brown sugar
    Nuts

An apple
A cold potato
Leftover berry pie

Boy does look better for it, true.
Sent him off to buy paper, pen, and ink. Half expect him to take money and disappear. Might be better for him if he did.

CHAPTER 3

On the morning of my second day as Nevery's apprentice, I woke up wrapped in my blanket, snug before the coal fire. My eye hurt a little from the day before, when Benet had thumped me, but it wasn't too bad. I could still see out of it.

Except for me, the room was empty. I

wriggled out of the blanket and headed for the door. Benet and Nevery were probably in the chophouse eating all the bacon. I headed downstairs.

Nevery and Benet were just gathering up their things. Oh, no. Had I missed breakfast? I skidded to a stop at the bottom of the stairs.

The wizard gave me one of his keen looks. Benet ignored me.

'All right, boy,' Nevery said, sitting down again. 'Eat quickly. I'll have another cup of tea.' Then he spoke to Benet. 'Pack up the things, and we'll leave straightaway.' Benet nodded and went off up the stairs.

The chophouse keeper brought stale biscuits from the day before, and some other things. I made a sandwich out of biscuit, jam, and cheese, and took a big bite.

Nevery poured himself more tea. Then he poured me a mug, too, and I took a drink, washing down my bite.

'Where we going?' I asked, and ate more biscuit sandwich.

He didn't answer right away. He was holding

a piece of paper, a letter, which he tapped a few times on the tabletop. Then, 'Heartsease.'

I opened my mouth to ask what that was, but he waved me silent. 'Just eat, boy. I'll answer your cursed questions before you ask them.' He drank his tea. 'Heartsease is a large mansion on its own island in the river. It is my home, but no one has lived in it for twenty years.'

I opened my mouth to ask another question.

'Don't ask why it's been empty that long,' he said. 'I ran into some trouble here in Wellmet some time ago, let that be enough.'

That was enough, for now. I nodded and took another bite of my breakfast.

'You may not have noticed,' he went on, 'but this city is facing a crisis. The level of magic has been dropping. Only ebbing, for years, but lately, I am told, the level has dropped more precipitously. If it is not stopped, Wellmet will fall into decay.'

'What're we going to do about it?' I asked.

He raised his bushy grey eyebrows. 'We? *I* am going to demand leadership of Magisters Hall so I can research the problem and then deal with it.' Nevery studied me for a moment. 'It could be dangerous.'

Well, I'd already figured that out. The magisters were unchancy enough, and he was dealing with Underlord Crowe, too.

He went on to explain how the balance of power worked in Wellmet. I knew it already but listened and ate while he explained. He got it mostly right. As I see it, the duchess, with help from her elected council, rules the city; she lives in the Dawn Palace on the east side of the river, what people call the Sunrise. Most of the fancy neighbourhoods, rich people, and fine shops are over there. Wizards keep it spelled and looking nice. You look like me, you don't go there in the daytime unless you want to spend some time in one of the duchess's fancy jail cells.

Then there is the Twilight, on the west side of the river. It's much smaller than the Sunrise because it's squeezed in where the river bends. In the Twilight are the mills and factories and warehouses. The Twilight is run by the Underlord. Crowe likes power and money, and he has minions to enforce his orders. He'd kill his own family to get what he wanted. Every thief, bagman, pickpocket, smokehole tavern owner – everyone – pays part of their takings to the Underlord. Kind of like taxes, except that the duchess's tax collectors don't bash you with clubs if you can't pay.

And in the middle of the river that winds through Wellmet are a chain of islands, and these are ruled by the magisters – the wizards.

Most of the time, three powers – magisters, duchess, Underlord – balance one another. All in all, not a bad system. If you live on the Sunrise side of the river.

Nevery was still talking, explaining Wellmet politics, while I finished my biscuit sandwich. I nodded to show him I was listening. As long as he kept talking, I could keep eating. I eyed the biscuits. Maybe one with butter this time. Mmm, and pickle. Sadly, there wasn't any bacon left.

'Are you paying attention, boy?'

I looked up from my plate. Nevery frowned, like he was about to turn me into a toad. I held my breath.

But then Benet came stomping down the stairs with his arms full of baggage. The wizard got to his feet, picked up his cane, and put on his wide-brimmed hat. He said to Benet, 'Give a few of those to the boy to carry and come along.'

I grabbed my buttered biscuit and went to the stairs to get the baggage from Benet. Ignoring me, he dropped two bags to the floor and followed Nevery from the room.

I looked at the bags: one for each hand. That left no hand for my biscuit. The chophouse door slammed – Nevery and Benet wouldn't wait for me, sure as sure. I took a big bite and shoved the rest of the biscuit into my pocket, picked up the bags – what did he have in there, rocks? – and ran out to the street.

Chewing, bag-dragging, I raced after Nevery and Benet. They turned a corner, and I had to run to catch up, headlong down Strangle Street, the bags bumping against my legs. It felt as though there was a big hand at my back, pushing me to catch up. With me panting after, we hurried through the Twilight. The air stank of open sewers and coal smoke and, as we got closer to the river, of dead fish and mud.

Nevery followed Shirttail Street down the hill until we got to the river, which might have a real name, but mostly people just called it *the river*. Here was the Night Bridge, which led over the river to the Sunrise, the duchess's part of the city.

The Night Bridge had houses built on it that looked like fat ladies hitching up their skirts as they crossed a brook. The brook, of course, was the river, and it roared beneath the ladies' skirts as it rushed along.

Nevery led the way onto the dark roadway between the tall houses. Halfway across the bridge, he turned down a narrow passageway between buildings.

Still lugging the bags, I followed Nevery and Benet down a covered stairway. I figured we'd come to the river, but we didn't; the stairs kept going down, ending at an arched stone tunnel.

Which led, I realized, to the magisters' islands in the middle of the river. A secret way! The tunnel was dark and smelled damp and fishy, like the river, and the stone-slabbed floor was wet and cold under my bare feet. Nevery held up his locus magicalicus and whispered a word, and his hand, holding the stone, burst into blue flame. I followed Nevery's flaming hand, which made shadows stalk along the arched stone walls. His cane made a muffled *tap tap* as we went along. After a short while we came to an iron gate that stretched across the passageway. Nevery spoke a few quiet, echoey words. The locus magicalicus sparked white for a moment, extended a finger of flame to the lock, and the gate clicked open.

One of these days, I decided, I would get myself a locus stone.

Nevery, Benet, and I went through, and the gate clicked closed behind me.

On we went through the twisty tunnels, until we came at last down a long, dripping passageway to another gate. Nevery raised the locus magicalicus. In the flickery blue light, I saw that this gate was rust-dusty and had cobwebs hanging from it. Something was chiselled in the stone under our feet; I could feel wet runes with my toes.

Nevery muttered a word. A key spell, like before, to open the gate. The locus stone sent out its finger of white light to the lock.

Nothing happened.

Nevery frowned and repeated the word again. Nothing.

My arms were tired. With a sigh, I dropped the bags onto the floor and sat on one of them.

'Be careful with those bags, boy,' Nevery said, not looking at me, but at the gate.

Right. But the bags hadn't been careful of me, had they? I opened one up and peered inside. Books. No wonder.

At the gate, Nevery knelt, looking closely at the keyhole.

I happened to be very good at picking locks. Well-known for it, actually. But the gate's keyhole was a funny shape, and I figured this kind of lock wouldn't open for me until I'd had more proper wizard training, so I didn't say anything. Nevery placed the locus magicalicus right up against the lock and shouted the opening spell.

An arrow of greeny-blue light shot from the

keyhole, knocked the stone from his hand, and burst into a shower of sparks that fell to the floor and sizzled in the puddles. With a long drone-groan, the gate opened, scraping across the stone floor.

'Come along,' Nevery said, after picking up his locus magicalicus. *Tap tap*, off he went down the passageway, Benet right behind him. I heaved up the bags and followed. The gate groaned closed after us.

The tunnel went on until we met a long stairway leading up. Nevery led us to the top, where he pushed a pile of browny-grey brambles out of the way and climbed out into the wintry grey light. Benet stopped at the top of the stairs, blocking me, so I squeezed around him to have a look.

Heartsease. It might once have been a grand, wide mansion house with rows of sparkling windows and columns out front, but that was a long, long time ago. Now it was a pile of soot-stained stone with dark, crack-paned windows, and a gaping hole that looked like somebody had taken a huge rock and dropped it right in the middle of the house where the double-wide doorway should be.

Two parts of the building were still standing, one on either side of the big bite taken out of the middle. Each one was four stories tall with a row of tiny windows just under the gap-tiled roof; chimneys stuck out the top like a row of snaggled teeth.

I loved it at first sight.

From the look on Nevery's face, he loved it, too, though I doubted he'd admit it. Benet just looked blank.

A courtyard lay before the house, filled with brambles and young trees sprouting right up through the cobbles. In the middle of the courtyard stood a huge, black-branched tree, but instead of leaves, the tree was crowded with coal-black birds. They perched, silent and still, along the branches, watching us with bright, yellow eyes. I had the feeling they'd been sitting there for a long time, waiting for something.

Nevery set off across the courtyard toward one of the parts of the mansion house left standing. As we approached the tree, the birds stirred and cackled quietly, talking about us. Nevery ignored them.

At the house, we were faced with an arched door hanging off its hinges. Nevery gave it a push with his hand and it creaked open. Within was a large, dark room stacked with dusty boxes and barrels and old broken furniture.

Nevery stood in the doorway, looking it over. 'Very well then,' he said. 'We'll start with this part of the house, Benet. My study first, then the rest of it. We'll have to clear all this out of here.' He glanced at me. 'Make yourself useful, boy.' He held out his hand. 'And give me the books.'

Gladly. I handed over the bags and Nevery picked his way across the room to a narrow stairway and went up, brushing cobwebs out of the way with his cane, each footstep raising a little puff of dust.

Leaving me with Benet. The muscle heaved up his luggage and started after Nevery. I followed, but at the bottom of the stairs Benet stopped and turned to me. I edged back out of his reach.

He pointed at the junk-filled room. 'Clean it.'

Well, I certainly wasn't going to argue with Benet. Following Nevery, he went up the stairs.

I looked over the jumble of junk in the room. Might as well get started. Boxes first, and then I'd haul the old chairs and tables and things outside, see what could be used and what was past saving.

I pulled the rotting wooden cover off one of the boxes and realized at once why Nevery had wanted me, his apprentice, to do this particular job.

Have moved back into Heartsease.

Eastern quarter of house is sound; four floors of it, at least.

Boxes of magical paraphernalia, books, even furniture in relatively good condition. House needs more work to be made livable, but good progress today.

CHAPTER 4

The box was full of magical things, all wrapped up in dusty silver paper. Another ten or eleven boxes were just the same. I wanted to unwrap them and find out what they were, but I figured Nevery would want to do it himself.

So I cleaned out the rest of the ground floor, dragging empty boxes and broken barrels out to the courtyard, and I found a mouse-chewed broom and started sweeping the cobwebs and mouse droppings from the walls and floors; the ceiling was too high to reach.

Then I went upstairs to find Nevery. He was on an upper floor, sitting in a dusty chair in a very dusty room reading an even dustier book.

'Nevery,' I said.

He looked up and snapped closed the book. A little cloud of dust flew up and he sneezed. 'What,' he said crossly, rubbing his nose.

'There's boxes of magical stuff downstairs. D'you want me to bring them up?'

'No,' Nevery said. 'Benet will do it.'

He went back to reading his book. I looked around the room. The high ceiling had plaster flowers and curlicues in the corners, all dust-crusted. The room contained a few other chairs, covered with faded, ripped cloth, and a long table with a scarred surface and heavy, carved legs. A threadbare carpet lay on the floor.

Leaning against one wall was an oil painting, about half as long as I was tall, with a tarnished gilt-gold frame around it. I crouched down to have a look. The paint was crusted over with dirt and smoke; maybe it had hung over a fireplace. I wiped away some of the cobwebs and dust that covered it.

'What is this, Nevery?'

'A painting,' he said without turning around.

Well, I could see that. 'A painting of what?' I asked.

'A dragon.'

I stepped back to look over the picture. 'It's a kind of animal?' I asked.

Nevery closed his book. 'You *are* ignorant, boy.'

I was, true.

'The dragon was a species of giant reptile,' Nevery said. 'Winged, horned, and crested, often with the ability to breathe fire.'

As he spoke, I saw, in the smoke and grime, the kind of creature he was talking about, just its outline.

'Dragons are extinct,' Nevery said. Before I could ask him what *extinct* meant, he said, 'It means they've all died out, boy. You won't ever see a dragon.' He opened his book again and nodded at the bookshelves that lined one wall of the room from floor to ceiling; they were all crammed with books and dust. 'Dust the shelves. Quietly. Let me read in peace.'

I found a cloth and got to it. The books were old and mouldy. I opened one to see what it looked like inside, and it made a crackly-crack sound that made Nevery look over at me and scowl. Carefully, I closed the book again, wiped it down, and put it back on the shelf. The cloth got dirty after a few minutes and I was covered with dust from my hair to my feet. But I kept working at it.

Finally Benet came back from whatever job he'd been doing and Nevery sent him down to fetch the boxes full of magical things.

'Put them here for now,' Nevery said, and Benet set down the box he was carrying and went downstairs for the rest. I went over to watch.

Nevery started by opening each box and handing me the tops, which I dumped in a pile by the door. Then he pulled one of the silver-paper-wrapped objects from the first box and unwrapped it.

Inside was a glass globe about the size of a fist. He held it up. In the greyish light, its surface glimmered with rainbows, like oil on water.

'What is it?' I asked.

'Scrying globe,' Nevery answered. 'You'll keep it polished. Use only wormsilk cloth or it will become clouded and unusable.'

I nodded. Right. I'd keep it polished. Good job for an apprentice.

Carefully, Nevery set the globe on the carpet beside his chair and unwrapped three more, each one larger than the next. I knelt down and peered at them. Scrying globes? 'What do they do?'

'Escry,' Nevery said.

That was not a very good answer.

He picked up the largest globe and examined it closely. Unlike the others, its surface was scorched black, as if somebody had toasted it with flames. He handed it to me. 'Useless,' he said.

Its surface felt gritty. I polished it on my sleeve, but it didn't get any cleaner. I wanted to look at it more carefully, but Nevery was unwrapping another object, a bowl made out of a turtle shell. Then he unwrapped a little tarnished silver knife in a leather sheath. After looking closely at the blade and testing it with his thumb, he tossed it aside, pronouncing it useless, so I picked it up and put it in my pocket. Next was a box of metal parts, tiny gears and pistons and springs, all of them rusty. 'Hmmm,' Nevery said. He handed the box to me. I put it next to my scorched scrying globe and gathered up an armful of crumpled silver paper and dumped it with the other junk by the door.

The first box empty, Nevery moved on to the next. The first thing he brought out and unwrapped was a small, dead alligator, stuffed, with glass eyes and yellow teeth. He regarded it for a moment, then handed it to me. 'Junk.'

I put it with the rest of my things. By this time I was hungry, and I pulled out the biscuit I'd stashed in my pocket and gnawed at it, watching as Nevery unpacked the rest of the boxes. Finally, he sat in his chair in the middle of the room, covered with dust and surrounded by magical things, empty boxes, and crumpled silver paper. He held a huge book from the last box.

The book had a worn leather cover and raggedy-edged pages and bulged with paper markers, dried leaves, diagrams in faded ink, fragments of maps – all bound together by a thick leather strap with a lock in it.

'Well, well,' Nevery muttered to himself. 'I thought they would have burned this.' He pulled out his locus magicalicus, whispered a spell word, and, with a little *pop*, the lock opened.

I leaned forward to watch, my biscuit forgotten.

My movement distracted Nevery, and he glanced over at me. 'You have work to do, boy. Go do it.'

Jumping to my feet, I shoved the half biscuit into my pocket, grabbed a cloth, picked up a book from the shelf, and wiped it down.

'Not in here,' Nevery growled. He nodded at the door. 'Out.'

I went.

We spent the rest of the day cleaning and moving into Heartsease. By nightfall, we were all tired and cold. Benet had found a chest full of moth-eaten blankets. I pinched a few of them, bundled up my burnt scrying globe, the box of gears, the stuffed alligator, and the painting of the dragon, and headed up to the top of the mansion house.

The ladder up to the attic was missing half its rungs, but I managed to climb to the top. I shoved my stuff up and poked my head through the trapdoor in the floor. The attic room was smaller than the others below, with a low, sloped ceiling and little windows with no glass in them, but it was snug enough. I climbed up and looked around. Except for me and my stuff, the room was empty. A thick layer of dust lay on the floor, and cracked plaster covered the walls. The room smelled of dust and dry rot.

I made a bed out of my blankets and snuggled up inside, nibbling at my biscuit. It had been a good, long day, and I was tired. I ate the last crumb and fell asleep.

Note to self: Boy's filthy rags make him look like gutterboy sneak thief. Which he is. But won't do to have servant of mine looking like that. Boy probably crawling with vermin, lice. Must give him few copper locks for new clothes and louse comb.

Weather cursed damp. Have caught nasty cold.

CHAPTER 5

I woke up on my third day as Nevery's apprentice hungrier than a pack of rats. The air blowing through the windows in my attic room was icy cold. I wrapped myself in one of the holey blankets, climbed down my ladder, and headed downstairs. The marble steps were freezing on my bare feet, and I was shivering by the time I made it to the second floor. Benet was there, building a wood fire in the wide fireplace.

He gave me a glare as I came in and pointed to a bucket standing by the stairs. He didn't say anything. He didn't need to – I knew what he wanted me to do.

I grabbed the bucket and scurried down the stairs and out to the well in the courtyard. The birds in the huge black tree watched me without stirring from their perches. After filling the bucket, I started to head back to the warm kitchen. Drats. Nevery would notice if I hadn't washed.

I went back to the well and, putting my bucket down, used the water in it to wash my face and neck and my hands and feet. Brrr. Even with my blanket wrapped around me, my teeth were chattering as I dipped the well bucket down, filled it again, and hurried back to the kitchen. There, Benet pointed to a kettle on the hearth, so I poured the water in, then huddled up next to the fire to get warm.

'Is there any breakfast?' I asked.

Benet didn't answer.

After a while, I got warm enough to look around. The room was not meant to be a kitchen. Maybe once it had been a drawing room, because it had tall windows and wallpaper and plaster flowers, just like Nevery's study upstairs. The fireplace was framed by white plaster ladies in draperies holding up a marble mantelpiece. Benet had moved in kitchen furniture – chairs and a sturdy table with a knife-scarred top and, by the hearth, a kettle, an iron trivet, and a three-legged stool. A closet door stood open; I guessed we'd use it for a pantry.

The kettle boiled. Benet took it off the fire and put it on the trivet, then added, from a small box on the table, a handful of tea leaves. When that had steeped for a while, he poured out the tea into a cup with a chipped gold rim and flowers painted on it. He gave me a glare and pointed up.

I got it: take the tea up to Nevery.

Leaving the blanket by the hearth, I brought the cup upstairs to Nevery's study. He was sitting in his dusty chair reading the fat book he'd found the day before.

I waited in the doorway until he looked up.

'Here's your tea,' I said.

'Well, bring it here,' Nevery said. He sneezed. The magical things were still scattered across the floor, so I picked my way across the room to his chair and gave him the tea. He took it and inhaled the steam rising up from the cup, then sneezed again and wiped his nose with a handkerchief. I went back to the door but hesitated before going out.

'What, boy?' he asked.

'Should I dust some more?' I asked.

He frowned at me.

'So you can stop sneezing,' I explained.

'I'm sneezing, boy, because I've caught a nasty cold.'

'You're sick?' I asked.

'Obviously I'm sick,' he said crossly. 'Surely you've had a cold once or twice; you know what it's like.'

A cold? I was cold all the time in the winter, but I'd never *had* a cold. I shook my head.

'Hmmm,' Nevery said. 'Ever had a stomach-ache? The runs? A fever?'

'No,' I said.

'You've never been sick, then. Odd. Very odd.' He set down his teacup. 'Come here.'

I picked my way back across the room and stood before him. He pulled my head down and looked through my hair.

'No vermin,' he said to himself. 'Hmmm.'

I stepped back.

Nevery looked me over. 'You're probably wondering about breakfast, boy.'

Yes, indeed I was.

'Go with Benet into the city. He will buy supplies and you will help carry them back here.'

All right. No breakfast because there was likely no food in Heartsease. I nodded and shivered back down to the fire in the kitchen. I only had a moment to get warm before Benet was ready to go. He led me down to the ground floor, stopped to put on a warm coat and stuff a string of copper locks in his pocket, and we were off.

I wondered how we were going to get through the magical gates, but Nevery had thought of that. Benet pulled from his pocket a small stone wrapped in a piece of cloth. It wasn't a locus magicalicus, because Benet wasn't a wizard, but something else not as powerful. He put the stone up against the lock and it clicked open.

We went on down the tunnel and through each of the gates, one after the other, until we came to the stairs leading up to the Night Bridge. Benet led the way and I followed, out onto the bridge and the busy morning traffic.

He turned left, toward the Twilight.

'We going to Sark Square?' I asked. Benet would be able to buy supplies there, cheaper than anyplace else in the Twilight. As we went along the dirty cobbled streets, I kept my eyes open. Underlord Crowe had a word out on me, which meant his minions would take me off the streets if they could get their hands on me.

But I didn't see anything that made me jumpy. Maybe it was too early in the morning for minions to be about.

I followed Benet up a twisting side street. Suddenly, he stopped, and I bumped into him. Glaring, he pulled out the string of copper locks

Nevery had given him, pulled off a few coins, and held them out to me.

I put my hands behind my back. What was he up to, giving me that much money?

He spoke without looking at me. 'Master Nevery says you're to get some new clothes.' He pointed at a shop door. 'Make it fast.'

New clothes! I grabbed the coppers and skiffed into the shop. It was a used clothing place, jammed full of bins of odd socks, stained petticoats, and patched shirts. Blinking in the dim light, I edged up to a rack of coats and pulled one out, holding it up to myself. Too big.

A hand came down on my shoulder. I looked around. The shop lady stood there, scowling. 'What d'you want here, boy?'

'Got anything else like this?' I asked, holding up the coat. 'But a little smaller?'

'Get out. I know your kind. You're a gutterboy.' She grabbed my arm, pulled me toward the door.

'No, I have money, see?' I jingled the coins in the palm of my hand.

She paused. I shook the money again. It made

a bright sound in the dark shop. She shook her head. 'All right, long as you've got money.'

Then she found me some warm trousers and socks and a shirt to go with the too-large coat, a woollen scarf, and a cap. And boots, I told her. Good stout boots for walking fast in. So I could keep up with Nevery.

The shopkeeper wanted to haggle, but I didn't have time – Benet had said to hurry. So I paid her price, took off my old rags, put on the new warm clothes, and laced up the boots. Stowing my knife and lockpick wires in my new coat pocket, I ran out to meet Benet.

He was standing outside the shop looking impatient.

The new clothes made me feel different, and not just less frozen. When I was dressed like a gutterboy, I felt like a gutterboy and sneaked around in the shadows. But wearing new clothes, it seemed like walking around in the daylight wasn't such a frightening thing. Well, I was the wizard's apprentice now, after all.

I still had one of the copper locks from the money Benet had given me, so when we got to

Sark Square, I stopped at a stall to buy – not steal! – a sausage in a biscuit, then ran to catch up with Benet.

'Want some?' I asked, holding out my breakfast. I was half afraid he'd take the whole thing, but he just ignored me, as usual.

We walked through Sark Square's market stalls and tents and their meager pickings. A few people, wrapped in rags and shawls, were shopping. At the end of one row of stalls stood an Underlord's minion holding a club, keeping an eye on things. My feet twitched and wanted to run, but my new apprentice clothes tricked him and his gaze slid right past me. I kept my head down, munching my biscuit, and followed Benet.

Using money Nevery had given him, he bought supplies, loading them into a wheelbarrow he paid a copper lock to rent.

I was curious about the keystone he'd used to unlock the gates in the secret tunnel, so when he was busy arguing with a stallkeeper about the price of eggs, I picked his pocket – *quick hands* – to have a look at it. The stone was grey and smooth, about the size of a thumbnail, and didn't seem magic in any way. I wondered how it worked. I wondered if it would open other locks, not just magical ones. I slipped it back into Benet's pocket as we walked to the next stall.

When the wheelbarrow was full, we headed back toward the Night Bridge. Fleetside Street snaked down to the river, and from the top of the steep hill I could see out across to the east side of Wellmet, the Sunrise, where the duchess ruled, and the streets were clean, and where I'd only been a few times, at night, to pick locks for burglars.

From where I stood I could also see out over the river to the chain of islands where Wellmet's wizards lived. The largest island, where the academicos was located, was just upstream from the Night Bridge. The academicos was a huge building topped with spires and towers. The next island was where the magisters had their meeting hall, which was fortified with a stone wall just above the waterline. Nevery's Heartsease was the most northern island in the chain. I pushed the hair out of my eyes to see better. The big hole in the middle of the mansion house's columns and windows looked like a bite out of a piece of cake.

I ran to catch up with Benet, and followed him back to Heartsease, I helped him drag the wheelbarrow up the stairs to the island; we were both panting with the effort by the time we got it to the top.

Benet unloaded the wheelbarrow, handing me things to carry up to the kitchen. After several loads, we were done and the kitchen was full of bags and boxes and packages. Benet stood looking at it all with his hands on his hips.

'Are we going to have dinner?' I asked.

Benet looked over at me and growled. I edged farther away from him in case he decided to thump me.

'You want to eat?' he said.

I nodded.

He pointed at the supplies. 'Then cook.'

Hmmm. I'd never cooked anything before. But I bet I could learn.

Weather turning colder. Early snow possible; could mean cold winter. River likely to freeze. My cold worse today.

Sent Benet and boy to Twilight for supplies. Heard them return. Had been studying grimoire, relearning embero spell. Went down to kitchen. Boy cooking dinner. Unsliced lump of bacon in a pan and potatoes charred in the coals. Potatoes half cooked, bacon raw in the middle. Tried a bite, then took pan from boy, sliced potatoes and bacon, and cooked them until properly done.

Boy asked how to make biscuits. Told him, but if they're anything like his potatoes, will be inedible.

Magisters meet tomorrow. Will send servant boy to spy on them, assuming embero spell works properly. Afterward, if he becomes too much trouble, will send boy away.

CHAPTER 6

The next morning, I mixed some biscuits the way Nevery had told me the night before. Flour, water, yeast, a little butter, and salt, all mixed up really well with a wooden spoon and plopped into a pan, which I put down into the fire's coals. Then I got out the other pan

and the bacon and got that started, and checked the kettle for water and swung it on its hook over the fire.

After a while, the biscuits turned browny black, so I took them off the fire. I tried one. It was like an egg. Hard and crusty on the outside, soft and runny on the inside. Not bad! I ate another one, with honey, and then had some bacon and some tea.

Benet came grumbling up the stairs. His hair was sticking up all over his head and he looked ferocious, like a bear. I stayed out of his way while he made himself tea. He put together a tray and took it up to Nevery in the study on the third floor.

When I'd finished my tea and got warm enough by the fire, I went up, too, and peeked in the doorway.

Nevery, looking fierce and red-nosed from his cold, was pacing before the hearth. He and Benet had been talking, clear as clear, and Benet, standing by the window, didn't look happy.

'Come in, boy,' Nevery said.

I went in. He hadn't eaten the biscuits, I

noticed.

'The magisters meet this morning,' he said.

Right. I nodded.

'Are you willing to be my spy at the meeting? It will require risking the embero spell.'

I nodded again. It was time for me to start doing wizardly things.

'I cannot predict what you'll become, boy,' Nevery said. 'The embero will change you into a creature characteristic to your nature.' He looked me up and down. He was, I could tell, trying to imagine what kind of animal I'd be.

'I'm not afraid, Nevery,' I said.

Benet, leaning against the wall with his arms crossed, made a growling sound.

I wondered if the change spell had been tried on him, and if it had, what kind of creature he'd become.

'Hmph,' Nevery grunted. 'We'll try it, then. You may go, Benet.' The muscle left the room, giving me an extra serving of glare before he went.

Nevery went to the table, where he studied a page in his grimoire for a few moments, muttering something under his breath, then slammed the book closed. After wiping his nose with his handkerchief, he reached into his pocket for his locus stone. 'Come here, boy,' he said. I went to stand before him. 'Do not resist the spell as it effects. It will hurt a little.'

A lot, he meant. But I wasn't worried.

'Now, keep still.' Nevery took a deep breath. Carefully, he laid the night-black locus magicalicus against my forehead. It felt soft and warm. Everything else in the room fell absolutely silent. Pressure built; my eardrums felt as if they were going to crack.

Then Nevery's voice rang out, spiralling through my ears and bouncing around in my skull. As he intoned the spell, the locus stone began to glow; he raised it over my head and sparks scattered, dash-flashing, surrounding us with a curtain of glittering light.

His voice grew louder, the words tumbling faster and faster from his mouth. My skin felt like paper lit on fire and my knees grew weak. I fell onto the floor. I saw a flash and heard a brief clap of thunder, and suddenly felt nothing at all.

After a while, I opened my eyes. Then closed them again. The room had gotten very tall; the chairs loomed overhead. Magic, sure as sure. Footsteps approached. Nevery's. I cracked my eyes open again. The wizard was bending over me, huge, reaching an enormous hand toward my head.

I yowled and leaped away; he, startled, fell backward onto the carpeted floor. I almost laughed, he looked so funny knocked back like that. But why was he so *big*?

He got to his feet. 'Boy,' he said. 'Come here and look at this.' He turned and brought a large flat square from the high table and set it on the floor.

I padded over to have a look.

Well. And I'd been afraid that my characteristic creature would be a cockroach or a mangy pipmouse. Clear as clear, Nevery had thought so, too.

But in the mirror I saw a midnight-black, skinny young cat with sparkling blue eyes and a quirked tail. It looked just like me. But furrier.

'It is you,' Nevery said, lifting the mirror

away. He sat in his chair and looked down at me. 'The embero spell effected remarkably easily, boy.'

Only half listening, I raised a paw and flexed, and sharp claws sprang out.

'The magisters' meeting is in an hour,' Nevery said.

I turned my head to examine the tail curving over my back. Amazing.

'Use that time to get acquainted with your new form. I have work to do.' He turned away and busied himself with papers at the table.

I remained still for a few moments. I practiced twitching my tail and swivelling my ears at every ristle-rustle of a turning page. A few dust motes sifted down from overhead and I felt a fierce urge to capture them and bear them squeaking and squirming to my den. I pounced, four-footed. My balance felt so sure; I couldn't fall if I tried. I leaped around the room, testing. It was the tail! It kept me perfectly balanced at all times. What fun! I practised prowling, making no sound. My black fur blended easily into the shadows at the edges of the room.

Oh, what a wonderful thief a cat would make!

I made another whirlwind tour of the room.

At the table, Nevery slammed down the book he had been reading. 'Perish it, boy, can't you keep still?'

I crouched down on my haunches and stalked his foot. Pounce!

He pulled away, frowning. 'Stop messing about. It's almost time for the meeting.'

He found his cane, put on his grey robe, and picked me up. As we walked through the dark, damp tunnels, he whispered instructions on what to look for and listen for. When we got to the Magisters Hall island, he opened the gate and set me down, nudging me with his foot to start me on my way. I twitched my tail and scampered off to steal some information.

Keeping to the shadows along the edge of the passages, the stone floor cold against my pawpads, I slunk into Magisters Hall. The meeting room was at the end of a long hallway, just as Nevery had said. But the door was closed. I padded up to it and crouched, listening. Voices, but no words. Drats.

I couldn't get in.

I slunk away and four-footed it back to the tunnel gate, and waited for Nevery. Soon he was there, wearing his grey robe and pacing. He scooped me up and swept-stepped back to Heartsease and up to his study.

As soon as the door closed behind him, he threw off his robe and wide-brimmed hat, pulled out his locus stone, and clapped his hands. Sparks flew. He grabbed up two handfuls of sparks and dumped them over my head. I felt the tingle, saw the flash of light, and heard the thunder.

Sometime later, when I opened my eyes, Nevery was standing over me. I sat up. I raised my hand. No more fur, no claws; I looked over my shoulder. No lovely quirked tail. I stretched and stood up, almost falling over. I missed the tail already.

'Now, boy, tell me about the meeting.' He sat down at the table and picked up his pen, ready to take notes.

Oh, he was not going to like this. 'Well, Nevery,' I began.

'Well, boy?'

I took a deep breath. 'I couldn't get in.'

He threw his pen onto the table; ink spattered. 'Curse it, boy. You'll have to go again after lunch.'

I nodded.

'And I expect you to get in, one way or another.' He pointed toward the door, scowling. 'Go tell Benet to give you something to do 'til then.'

As I went out, I heard him mutter, 'Useless.'

Hearing him say that gave me a hollow, empty feeling in my stomach.

Blasted boy. Sent him to listen in at Magisters Hall, came back with nothing.

Embero spell had odd effect, though.

Note to self: must read Sarpent's historical grimoires to see if he notes this kind of effect. Generally, undergoing embero not a pleasant experience. Last attempted this spell on Benet. Disaster. Boy seemed to enjoy it.

Consider possibility that because boy has touched locus magicalicus, it has developed an affinity to him? Odd sort of adosyncratichi. Warrants further investigation.

Note to self: Do not allow boy to cook; have Benet do it.

CHAPTER 7

When we finished lunch, I lugged up some water for washing and joined Benet in the kitchen. He'd made tea and a basket of muffins for afters. I sniffed at the basket. 'Smells good,' I said.

Benet sat with his chair tipped back against the wall. He held knitting needles and had a pile of black wool next to

76

his chair; the needles went *tick-click-tick*. He didn't answer.

Oh, well. 'D'you want another?' I took one of the muffins and held the basket out to Benet. He ignored it.

Putting the basket down, I bit into my muffin and washed it down with a gulp of tea.

Benet watched me but didn't speak. His knitting needles flashed, quick and silver in the black wool.

I ate the last muffin and drank more tea. Then I picked up the crumbs from the bottom of the empty muffin basket and ate those.

'What's it like, then, you,' Benet said, 'being a cat?'

I froze. Benet had spoken to me. I looked at him, but he didn't seem angry: not a glare to be seen. 'Well,' I said slowly, 'it's . . . hard to explain.' I wasn't sure I could even explain it to myself. 'The tail is amazing.'

'Didn't hurt?' Benet asked. 'The spell?'

No more than changing clothes hurt. 'No.'

He gave me a glare, just a little one. 'Reckon you're lying.'

I looked at him. So he'd been hurt when Nevery'd tried the spell on him.

'Could use a cat around here,' Benet said. 'Storeroom's full of mice.' He put the snarl of black wool and his knitting needles on the floor and got to his feet. 'Master Nevery wants you.'

I jumped up. 'I'm ready.' I followed Benet upstairs to the study. The remains of Nevery's muffins and tea lay on the table and a merry fire burned in the hearth.

Nevery himself sat at the table, his grimoire open before him. When I came in, he narrowed his eyes and frowned. Yes, I knew I had to get the information he needed or I'd be in big trouble.

Nevery got to his feet. 'All right, boy,' he said, and held up his locus magicalicus. I stepped forward. He checked the grimoire one last time, placed the stone against my forehead, and did the thing with the sparks and the ringing incantation.

This time I listened more carefully so I could remember the words of the spell. That's what a wizard's apprentice is supposed to do: learn spells. But I didn't get all of it before everything went black and silent.

When I woke up, Nevery was seated at the table, working. I stretched. Then I took a padding tour of the room. When I got around to Nevery, I sat in front of him, curling my tail over my paws. He ignored me.

I sighed and lay down to wait.

Finally, Nevery stood up. 'The magisters should be done with their lunch by now.' He picked up his cane and put on his wide-brimmed hat. 'And this time, boy, you'd better come away with more than a closed door.'

Yes, all right. He put on his robe, I leaped up into his arms, and we left.

As I had that morning, I padded down the stone passageways to the meeting room. This time the door was opened, and I went in.

In the dim room, the magisters sat around a long table, a fat wizard at its head. None of them noticed me sneak in. I crouched at the base of the fat wizard's chair, in shadows, and pricked up my ears. They were talking about the weakening flow of magic to the system of werelights that lit the eastern part of the city, the Sunrise.

The fat magister's name was Brumbee. He had a round, rosy face and was dressed in bright yellow wormsilk and velvet robes over a plain black suit and waistcoat. The sleeve of his robe had a patch with a fat black-and-yellow-striped bee embroidered on it. With my paw I patted his pocket. He kept a locus stone in there, and a ring of keys. I couldn't get them out to look at them because cats might be good prowlers, but they're not very good at picking pockets.

I was just settling into the shadows beside his chair for a good listen when Brumbee's big, gentle hands reached down, picked me up by the middle, and set me on his lap. I struggled, but he held me tightly by the scruff, then gave me a scritch behind the ears. 'Nice kitty,' he murmured in a soft voice.

He was all right, then. I sat down, tail-over-paws, ready to pick up some information to bring back to Nevery.

At last the magisters finished their discussion of the werelights.

'Very well then,' Brumbee said. He reached into his other pocket and pulled out a delicious-smelling napkin. Then he unwrapped it – a sandwich left over from his lunch! – and fed me a sliver of chicken. I ate it and licked my whiskers. 'I am afraid that I must again bring up the problem of the decay of magic in Wellmet.' Brumbee looked down the table at the other wizards. 'The duchess expects us to act to deal with this situation. And we don't want things to spin out of our control.'

'I agree that the situation is becoming alarming,' said a lady wizard with grey hair piled in a messy bun atop her head. 'And that we need someone to focus his or her attention on dealing with this crisis. What about you, Brumbee? Would you do it?'

The fat wizard shook his head. 'No, no, Periwinkle. *I* don't want to do it. What about you, Sandera?'

A keen-looking, youngish woman at the other end of the table shook her head. 'Oh, indeed no, Brumbee. Not I. But we do, as you know, have another choice.' She looked around the table.

'Not Pettivox,' the grey-haired Periwinkle said.

Brumbee shook his head. 'Certainly not. I purposely did not invite him today so we could consider the matter without him. Pettivox would not be suitable.'

'Power hungry,' Sandera agreed. 'Therefore he is a danger, don't you know. And he spends too much of his time travelling to the desert city. But there is still one more to consider.'

A tall, sharp wizard banged his bony fist and glared down the table at Brumbee. 'We cannot name Nevery!'

Brumbee raised his eyebrows. '*I* didn't mention Nevery.'

'Well, you were thinking of him,' the sharp wizard said. 'I could tell. Now, we all know he's managed to get the order of exile repealed and has returned to Wellmet. And we all know why.'

The grey-haired wizard nodded her head. 'True enough. Nevery has returned. But I don't see that asking him to lead us magisters through this crisis would be such a bad thing. Better than

Pettivox, certainly.'

The sharp wizard groaned. 'Nevery is dangerous. He pays absolutely no attention to the laws governing the use of magic in the city. He will lead us into trouble. He's already dealing with the Underlord, I hear.'

The fat wizard gave me a reassuring stroke. 'Not to worry. I think everyone realizes that in such times as these, we need a wizard like Nevery. He is the only one who can balance the Underlord and the duchess. And despite his hastiness, he's the finest wizard this city has ever seen.'

'I agree, Nevery would be best,' said Periwinkle.

'I concur,' added the keen lady, Sandera.

'Well, Trammel?' Brumbee asked.

'Oh, all right,' the sharp wizard answered. 'But don't think I'm going on my knees to Nevery's ghastly old mansion to beg him to lead us.'

'That's all right, Trammel,' Brumbee said. His fingers tapped me twice on the head. *Pay attention*, he seemed to be saying. I sat up. 'I have a feeling that Nevery will come to us.' He nodded. 'He will meet with us soon. And, I think, that concludes the meeting.' The other wizards began to rise, talking, shuffling papers.

Right. I had what I needed. I got ready to spring from Brumbee's lap, to race to tell Nevery the news. The wizard's big hand stopped me. 'Off you go now, kitty.' The man smiled and gave me another rub under the chin. In spite of myself, I purred. 'Run back to your master, as fast as you can.'

I leaped from the wizard's lap and tore out of the magisters' meeting chamber.

CHAPTER 8

Back at Heartsease, Nevery changed me into a boy, and I told him what the magisters had said. That they were worried about the ebbing magic crisis, that the wizard Pettivox wanted the job of leading them, but that the magisters knew Nevery was in Wellmet, that they wanted him to lead them instead. 'All you have to do is ask,' I told him.

'I can draw my own conclusions, boy,' Nevery said sharply. He got up from his chair and paced across the room, then back again. 'And they all agreed not to support Pettivox?' he asked.

I nodded. 'Sandera said he was power hungry.'

'Pettivox is a decent wizard. But he's a terrible leader. Hmmm. Things must be worse than I thought for them to offer it to me so readily. I wonder if I was too hasty, going to the Underlord.' He put his hands behind his back and paced some more, muttering into his beard.

Coming to a turn in his pacing, he noticed that I was still there. 'Well, go on out, boy.' He gestured for me to leave the room.

I took two steps toward the door. Then stopped. 'Nevery?' I asked.

He paused in his pacing and scowled. 'What, boy?'

'I was just wondering when I'm going to learn tricks like that.'

'Tricks? What are you talking about?'

'Well, Nevery, I am your apprentice. I'm supposed to learn the embero spell, right? I've got all of it except for the end, and I need the rest.'

Nevery shook his head, and his scowl deepened. 'Don't be stupid, boy. You are not my apprentice. I took you on as a servant, nothing more.'

Not his apprentice? I stared at him. Something strange was happening to my stomach, like the bottom was falling out of it and a giant black pit opening up. Not his apprentice, after all. His servant.

I wasn't sure I could be a servant, not even for Nevery.

Without saying anything, Nevery got up and went to the table, fetched his grimoire, and sat down again. He opened the book and marked a spot on the open page. He cleared his throat. 'All right, boy. Tell me the embero spell.'

I swallowed down the lump in my throat. 'It goes *tumbriltumbrilulartambefranjevaneekhouten-franjelickavanfranjelocar*' – I paused to take a breath – *'franjelilfraajellumiolendilarterkolil*—'

'*Tark̲olil*,' Nevery corrected, looking up from the book.

'Right, *tarkolil*,' I said, *'lilotarkolilotar-kennan ...'* I stopped. 'That's all, then everything goes black.'

There was a long silence. Finally, Nevery nodded and closed the grimoire. 'The spell won't effect unless the magic is focused and released with a locus magicalicus. But that's all of it, boy.'

Oh. Well, it didn't matter now.

Might as well get it over with. 'I wouldn't be a very good servant, Nevery. So . . . so thanks for turning me into a cat. And showing me Heartsease.' I stared down at my feet so I wouldn't have to look at him. I turned to leave the study.

'Wait,' Nevery said. I stopped with my back to him. 'You'd rather go back to thieving on the streets of the Twilight than serve me?' He sounded angry.

I thought about it. I was a good thief, and an even better lockpick. Most of the time I did all right. Most of the time I managed to avoid being noticed by the Underlord and his minions. But sometimes, no matter how hard I scrambled, things got bad. I'd go hungry for a few days, or the weather would get cold and I wouldn't have a copper lock for a corner in a crowded cellar to sleep in, or I'd have to fight off a stray misery eel, or somebody would steal my shoes.

Working for Nevery would be easier. I wouldn't mind sweeping and polishing scrying globes and fetching water if I were his apprentice. But I couldn't do it as his servant. Not even if it meant going back to the Twilight.

I shook my head and headed for the door.

'Wait,' he said again. I stopped, but I still didn't turn around. 'All right.' He sighed. 'Maybe I do need an apprentice.'

Suddenly everything looked a lot brighter. I turned back to him.

'All well then, boy?' Nevery asked.

Outside, at that moment, the sun came out and shone straight in the window, and a beam of light splashed me right in the face. I blinked, dazzled. The room was flooded with afternoon sunlight, thick as honey, but brighter, sweeter. Dust motes danced in the air like tiny stars. I realized that I was grinning. 'All right, Nevery,' I answered.

'Yes, all right, boy,' Nevery said gruffly. 'Go and get yourself some dinner.'

Never had an apprentice, never wanted one. Still don't want one. Not a good teacher, for one thing, and don't want apprentice underfoot. Boy very likely to be more trouble than he's worth.

No locus magicalicus (serious problem)
Habitual liar, thief, etc.
Eats cupboards bare
Aggravates Benet

On the other hand, boy's abilities of interest. Can't think of any wizard who could have repeated a twice-heard spell as difficult as the embero, but boy did it. Very surprised. Also, odd that boy has never been ill, despite living on streets as gutterboy. Possibly has some affinity with city's magic. Though no precedent for such a thing.

Note to self: Send Benet out for materials to build gauge for measuring ambient level of magic. Must determine whether, as has been claimed, the rate of magical decay is increasing.

List for Benet:

    Copper wire, springs
    Optical lenses (panvex, pancave)
    Slowsilver (as much as he can get)
    Verity crystal (dark one, if possible)
    Dock pendulums (three)
    Burnishing powder
    Partelet
    Nuts, bolts, screws of various sizes
    And more food. Boy eating pantry bare.

CHAPTER 9

I'd never been into Nevery's workroom before. It was where he prepared his magics. He'd had Benet rip down the tattered wallpaper and whitewash the walls, and he kept werelights burning in a crystal candelabra hanging from the ceiling, so it was bright in there, and clean, but not tidy. In the centre of the room was a high table covered with alembics and copper coils, dirty teacups, scrying globes, bits of silk cloth, and papers. And in the middle of the table, a jumble of brown-paper-wrapped parcels.

In the morning, when I came in the door with tea and a plate of biscuits and honey, Nevery was perched on a high stool at the table. He looked up at me and lowered his bushy grey eyebrows into a scowl.

'Knock first, boy,' he said. 'You made me spill the slowsilver.'

Sure enough, a few flowing silver balls snailed their way down the table and oozed to the floor.

'I'll get them!' I put down the tea and biscuits, grabbed a glass jar from the high table, and went after the slowsilver.

'Stop!' Nevery roared, leaping up from the stool. I froze. He leaned over and snatched the jar from my hand. 'Look, boy.' He showed me the jar. Greenish crystals crusted the inside. 'Tourmalifine,' he said. 'Slowsilver cannot mingle with tourmalifine.'

I looked at the jar, then at the slowsilver snails on the floor. 'Why not?'

'Because when mingled they explode.' He

polished a different jar with his sleeve and handed it to me. 'Now, pick up the slowsilver. Carefully. It's cursed hard to come by, and I need every drop.'

I went down on my knees under the table and chased the slowsilver around while Nevery sat on his stool drinking tea and eating his breakfast. Slowsilver was tricky, I found, because I couldn't actually pick it up. It squirmed away from my fingers and split into tinier snails. The best way to collect it was to blow on it to get it oozing along, then scoop it up with the glass jar. Of course, then the slowsilver I'd already caught tried to get out again.

I wondered what slowsilver was for, since the white-haired wizard at the Underlord's mansion had wanted more of it.

'Nevery,' I said, coaxing a shiny-bright snail into the jar. 'Why can't slowsilver and tourmalifine mingle?'

'I already told you, boy. They explode.'

'Yes, but why?' I caught the last bit of slow-silver and crawled out from under the table. Standing, I put the glass jar on the table, but far away from the jar of tourmalifine. I leaned over to look closely at the slowsilver. It looked like a shiny puddle of mirror, swirling gently, peacefully. 'What is it about slowsilver and tourmalifine? When they're alone they don't explode. So why do they when they're together?'

Nevery finished off his tea and put down the cup. He nodded, pulling on the end of his beard. 'Yes. It's not a bad question, boy.' He stood up. 'Come with me.'

I followed him out of the workroom and down to the study, where he pulled from a shelf a fat book bound in red leather.

'Here.' He put the book into my hands. 'Read the fifth chapter, which will answer your question, and then I will test your understanding of it.'

'But—'

Nevery scowled. 'One thing you'll have to learn, boy, if you're to be my apprentice. You don't argue with me. Just do as you're told.' With that, he swept out of the room, slamming the door behind him.

I went to the table, sat down, and opened the

book. Hmmm. The pages were brittle with age and brown around the edges. The ink was bright, though, and diagrams in different colours decorated almost every page. I closed it and got up to walk around the room for a while.

Clear as clear, Nevery was busy with something in his workroom and didn't want to be bothered.

Well then, I wouldn't interrupt him. Ever since we'd come to Heartsease, I'd been wanting to explore the other part of the mansion.

I left the study and went outside. In the courtyard, the wind was blowing and, overhead, dark grey clouds raced across a lighter grey sky. The clouds were full of rain. Not snow; it wasn't quite cold enough.

Picking my way through the brambles, I went around the side of the house until I came to a place where I could climb through a window to get inside. The window was about twice my height from the ground, but a thick vine of ivy grew up the wall and around it, so I climbed up that way. The panes were broken. Clinging to the vine with one hand, I reached in, unlatched the window, pushed up the sash, and slid inside.

It was a workroom. I blinked, my eyes adjusting to the dim light, and saw that rain had gotten in the broken window; the curtains and the carpet were damp and rotten. It smelled of mildew. It had a high table and stools, and walls lined with shelves. On the table were lots of glass jars and alembics, all clouded with dust and cobwebs.

And some sort of little metal machine about as big as my hand, with cogs and pistons that looked melted, like it had been struck by lightning. I put it in my coat pocket to show to Nevery.

And then I found the interesting things.

At one end of the room was a wooden desk, fancy and carved. Underneath it was a locked chest, banded with metal, dusty and cobwebby.

I dragged out the chest from under the desk and used my coat sleeve to wipe it off. The lock looked basic, a simple four-pin double crick-twister. I pulled out my lockpick wires. I knew – *knew* – I should wait for Nevery to open it. But I couldn't wait. I had to know what was in there.

Kneeling before the chest, I bent the wires into the right shapes and slid them into the lock. *Quick fingers*, and the wires clicked right into place and the lock turned over. Easy. Almost like it wanted to be opened. I pulled the wires out of the lock, put them in my pocket, and opened the squeaky lid of the chest.

It was full of rocks.

From Nevery Flinglas, Wizard,
to the Wellmet Magisters.

My former colleagues, you are no doubt aware
that I have returned to Wellmet; I am able
to inform you that the order of exile that
banished me from the city twenty years ago
has been lifted, by order of Her Grace, the
duchess.

The city, I judge, is suffering from a
magical decay; I expect you have noticed.

My assessment is that the wizards of
Magisters Hall need someone to guide
them first towards an understanding of the
situation and then in creating a plan to deal
with the decay of magic. I offer my services
and hereby volunteer to serve as your leader
during this crisis.

When you have discussed my offer, you may reply to me at Heartsease.

NEVERY FLINGLAS

CHAPTER 10

The rocks I'd found were laid out on trays covered with faded blue velvet, the trays stacked five deep to the bottom of the chest, where I found a book covered with cracked leather and stamped with gold runes and an hourglass with wings at its sides. I'd seen the same hourglass before, carved into the stone floor by the gate leading to Heartsease, and on the patch on Nevery's robe.

I set the book aside, then lay the trays around me on the floor and inspected the rocks. The first one was grey, flat, and rounded, a river stone about the size of my palm. When I touched its smooth surface, it felt warm and strangely welcoming. I closed my eyes and a picture flashed into my mind of a tall, slender, grey-haired lady in a grey gown. She raised her hand, which held the grey, flat stone, and then faded away.

The next rock was a rough black lump with chunks of cloudy crystal embedded in it. I picked it up and saw a burly, bearded man who reminded me of Nevery. He scowled at me, and I put the rock down on its bed of velvet.

The next was a slim shard of bluish crystal. I touched it and caught a glimpse of a young girl with blonde hair and a quick, shy smile, who turned and flitted away, out of my vision.

Sitting on the mouldy carpet of the workroom, I examined every one of the stones. Some were empty, as if every drop of magic had been poured out of them like water. Some made the tips of my fingers tingle, and some gave a single warm throb and went still and quiet again, as if falling back to sleep.

The last stone was wrapped in a scrap of yellowed wormsilk tied up with a frayed ribbon. When I picked up the little package to unwrap it, it felt light, as if nothing was inside, though I could feel the smoothness of stone beneath the silk. Carefully, I untied the ribbon and the stone rolled out of the cloth and into my palm.

As it dropped into my hand, a cold wave of sickness rolled out from it, washing through me, making my stomach turn over and dark spots dance before my eyes. The stone shoved me, *away*. Dropping it, I scrambled backwards until I crouched in the doorway, shivering.

It lay there on the floor. I gripped the doorframe and caught my breath. From where I was, the stone looked like a polished gemstone, about the size of a baby's fist. I crept closer to see it better, kneeling to look it over, but not touching it. The stone was deep purple, like a black eye, but as I looked closer I saw that it was covered with fractures that went right through it. Really, it was more cracks than stone. I'd have to tell Nevery about it.

Leaving it on the floor, I put the other stones back into the chest, keeping the book out to show to Nevery. As I was closing the lid of the chest, I caught, out of the corner of my eye, something moving in the room.

I whirled around to look – thinking the bruise-coloured stone had decided to attack me again.

But it wasn't the stone. It was a cat.

She sat just inside the doorway, looking at me with yellow-green eyes. Her face and tail were striped with dark grey and black and the rest of her was white, as if somebody had held her by her tabby ears and tail and dipped her in bleach. She looked sleek and well fed.

The tip of her tail twitched. I knelt down beside her and gave her a scratch in the soft fur between her ears. She gave me a purr and rubbed her little face against my hand.

'D'you want to come with me, Miss?' I asked.

I fetched the cracked-leather book, which I

put in my coat pocket, along with the strange melted-metal machine, and headed to the window. The cat followed me up onto the windowsill, where I crouched, looking out.

Outside, the rain had started, a chill downpour, a grey curtain across the courtyard. I jumped down, my boots squelching as I hit the ground, and the cat went primly down the vine.

'Well done, Lady,' I said. 'D'you want me to carry you so you don't get wet?' I bent down and picked her up, sheltering her under my coat.

I ran across the courtyard, pelted by the rain, splashing through puddles. Near the storeroom door stood a huge, wet pile of firewood; Benet must have chopped it. I ran past that and into the storeroom.

Dripping wet, I went up to the kitchen. Benet was there, at the table, cutting up a chicken with a long knife.

He paused as I came in. 'He's looking for you,' he said, pointing with the knife at the ceiling.

I nodded and put the cat down. She sneezed and stalked away from me. Maybe she thought the rain was my fault. 'Her name is Lady,' I said. 'She's very good at catching mice.'

Benet grunted. 'And he isn't happy.'

No, I wouldn't expect him to be.

Slowly I went up the stairs to the study. As I came in the door, Nevery looked up from a book, then stood up. He slammed the book down on the tabletop. I froze with my hand on the doorknob.

'I gave you an assignment, boy,' he growled, 'to read the fifth chapter, and you disobeyed.'

'No, I didn't,' I said. Well, I hadn't. Not really.

'Have you read this?' He pointed at the red leather book, which was still sitting open on the table.

'No,' I said.

Nevery looked like mingled slowsilver and tourmalifine. 'You haven't read it.'

I took a deep breath. He wasn't going to like this. 'Nevery, I don't know how to read.'

The wizard stared at me. Shook his head. Muttered something under his breath. Then he asked, 'You've had no schooling at all?'

I stared back at him. I'd grown up in the Twilight, he knew that. Where would I have had schooling?

Nevery sat down again. 'Well then, boy. *I* don't have time to teach you to read. You'll have to go to the academicos.'

To school?

Nevery lowered his eyebrows. 'Don't argue, boy.'

No, I wasn't going to argue. I was going to school.

CHAPTER 11

I gave Nevery the book I'd found in the other workroom and told him about the chest full of stones. I also showed him the little melted-metal device.

He turned it over in his hands, poking at its springs and frozen cogwheels.

'What is it?' I asked.

'Magic capacitor,' he said, setting the device on the table.

'What's a capacitor?'

He shot me an impatient look from under his eyebrows and picked up the device again. 'See this bit, here?' He flicked at a finger-wide tube that opened like a grinning mouth. 'Intake valve. Ambient magic is sucked in, there.' He poked at a plump metal bulge. 'And stored here. Slowsilver restrains the magic. A wizard can then examine and test the stored magic before releasing it again, through this valve, here.' He poked at a little flywheel, then handed the device to me.

It was heavier than it looked. I didn't like it.

'You're cursed nosy, boy,' Nevery said. After growling at me a bit more for going into the other part of the mansion, Nevery handed out his punishment for what he called nosiness and I called ordinary curiosity: he made me carry the pile of wood Benet had chopped into the storeroom, where it would be out of the rain and easier to fetch in the mornings when Benet needed wood for the kitchen fire.

When I finished that, I went back into the study. Nevery sat in his chair, reading the book with the winged hourglass on the cover.

'I'm all done with the wood,' I said. While I'd worked, the rain had continued, so my clothes were wet, and I was cold and a little tired. I edged closer to the hearth, where a fire burned merrily.

He didn't look up from the book. 'Good. Now go and find something else to do.'

'Actually, Nevery,' I said, holding my chilled hands before the flames, 'I wanted to talk to you about the stones.'

He closed the book with a snap. 'The stones you found in the workroom.'

I nodded and sat down, cross-legged, on the hearth. 'They're locus magicalicus stones, aren't they?' I said.

'Of course they are,' Nevery said. He paused for a moment. 'The wizards who possessed them are all long dead.' He held up the book. 'This is my family chronicle. Their names and the descriptions of the stones are recorded here.'

'Oh,' I said. I stared into the fire. So the

scowling, bearded man in the rough rock and the shy girl in the sliver of blue crystal were gone.

Nevery gave me his keen-gleam look. 'Well, boy? I suppose, given your nosiness, you examined the stones.'

'Yes.' I sighed. 'I liked the grey lady best.'

'The grey lady,' Nevery repeated.

'The one in the flat river stone. She had a good smile.'

Nevery leaned forward in his chair and grabbed me by the chin, turning my face toward him. 'Are you lying to me, boy?' he asked fiercely.

I blinked and tried to pull away, but he held me tightly.

'*Are* you?' he repeated.

'No!' I said.

He let me go and sat back in his chair, glaring down at me.

I scrabbled away, just out of his reach.

'You didn't read about the stones and their bearers in the book, did you?'

'No, Nevery,' I answered. 'I saw them when I touched the stones.'

'Hmph,' Nevery said. 'Did you. Very

interesting. Tell me about them.'

All right. I told him about every one of the stones, and what I'd felt or seen when touching each one. He interrupted me a few times to consult the book, then nodded and told me to continue. I told him about the bruise-purple jewel stone, how it had attacked me.

'I'm not at all surprised,' Nevery said, 'given what it was. My great-great-aunt Alwae's jewel stone. You were lucky it didn't do worse.'

I'd finished telling about the stones. We sat in silence for a while, me looking at the fire, him paging through the book.

Nevery cleared his throat. 'As you have probably gathered, the locus magicalicus reflects the nature of its bearer. A weak wizard has a soft stone, easily broken, and will go to great lengths to protect it. The stone of a strong-willed wizard is hard.'

Ah. Nevery's stone, I remembered, was very hard and smooth, polished, almost like a mirror. And very, very dangerous. Its ice and wind had almost killed me after I'd stolen it from Nevery's pocket.

He paused and glanced at me. 'Are you listening, boy?'

I nodded, and he continued.

'Sometimes a wizard's stone is no more than a common pebble picked up from the side of the road. Sometimes it is a fine jewel like Alwae's stone, but such a stone appears only very rarely and with dire consequences. The locus magicalicus, after the wizard has possessed it for some time, can take on aspects of its bearer. And after the wizard's death, the stone remains imbued with his or her nature.'

'Can a stone ever be destroyed?' I asked.

'Hmmm. It could, yes. If the wizard attempted magic greater than the stone could bear. In that case, the wizard would certainly die as well.'

It was all very interesting, and he was telling me these things because I really was his apprentice now. We sat quietly for a little while. Lady came in and, after sniffing at Nevery's foot, climbed into my lap. I stroked her and stared at the fire, leaning against the side of Nevery's chair. The room was warm, and the chill I'd gotten from shifting the wood had been all baked out by the fire. All I needed now was some dinner, but I couldn't be bothered to move to get it. Lady purred.

'What's this?' Nevery said, closing the locus stone book.

What? I looked up, blinking. Had I fallen asleep? Lady climbed off my lap and stretched.

Nevery pointed at her.

'A cat,' I said.

'I can see that,' Nevery said. 'What is it doing here?'

'She lives here,' I said. He frowned, so before he could decide he didn't want Lady around, I said, 'Benet said we need her for the mice.'

'Hmmm. Perhaps we do.' He set the book aside and got to his feet. 'Well, boy. You will have to find yourself a locus magicalicus. The sooner the better. And tomorrow we go to the academicos.'

Boy has interesting ability. Very sensitive to locus magicalicii. Can read stones. Saw my mother in her stone; called her the grey lady.

No response yet from magisters to my letter. No doubt they are debating the wording of the first sentence — and having accomplished so much, will go on to discuss what to have for supper.

CHAPTER 12

N every decided to take me to the academicos the next afternoon because he'd heard the magisters were meeting later in the evening.

'They won't be expecting me already,' he

said, picking up his cane and jamming his wide-brimmed hat onto his head. 'Best to keep them on their toes. Come along, boy.'

He swept out of the mansion and, me following, went across the puddled courtyard, then down the stairs to the tunnel and the gate. Without hesitating, he raised his locus magicalicus and spoke the opening spell. After a sputter and spark, the gate swung open and he strode through it, me running to keep up.

'Nevery,' I said, wanting to ask him about how to find a locus stone and also about going to school. They were going to teach me to read, of course, but what else?

'Listen, boy,' Nevery said, pausing to give me one of his keen-gleam looks, then striding on.

I nodded to show him I was listening.

'You must call me "Master", not "Nevery".'

I didn't get it. Nevery was his name, wasn't it? 'Why?' I asked.

'It's a sign of respect, boy.'

'I respect you,' I said. It was true; I did.

He shook his head. 'It shows that you respect that I possess knowledge, experience, and abilities that you do not, boy. That I am your master.'

I thought about that while Nevery opened one of the gates. 'But I possess knowledge, experience, and abilities that you do not, Nevery.' And at least I didn't call him *old man* the way he called me *boy*.

'Perhaps. But I am your teacher,' Nevery said.

'Well,' I said, running a few steps to catch up with him, 'I could teach you what I know, if you like.'

'Could you indeed?' He shot me another look. 'What, for example?'

'Like picking pockets and locks, learning the secret ways in the city, walking in the shadows. It's worth knowing.'

He looked like he was about to answer, then he closed his mouth and strode on, his cane going *tap tap tap* on the damp cobblestones of the tunnel. He let us through another gate, polished and more ornate than all the other gates. 'Hrm,' he said. 'This is the academicos gate. Come along.'

He led the way up the stairs to the

academicos island. The stairs opened onto a wide flagstone-paved courtyard thronging with chattering students and teachers. The school itself was a huge central building with four spired towers that were flanked by four-storey wings that reached out like embracing arms.

As Nevery strode across the courtyard, me hurrying behind him, people stopped and stared and gathered in little groups to point him out as he passed along. He ignored them; knowing Nevery, he didn't even notice. When we reached the wide steps leading up to the academicos front door, he *tap tap*ped toward the door, then turned aside, seeing someone he recognized.

Oh, no. I recognized him, too. The fat wizard from Magisters Hall. I felt suddenly afraid that he wasn't going to want me at his academicos.

'Brumbee,' Nevery said with a nod.

Brumbee, who wore the same dark suit under the bright yellow robes I'd seen him in before, looked surprised. 'Nevery!'

'The magisters meet this evening, do they not?' Nevery asked.

'Yes, we do.' Brumbee blinked. 'Perhaps we

should go into my chambers to, ah, discuss it?'

'No,' Nevery said. 'I have a few things to do before the meeting.'

'Oh! Then you'll be joining us?' Brumbee asked.

'Yes,' Nevery answered. He pointed at me. 'This boy here is my, hrm, apprentice. He needs a place at the academicos.'

'Your apprentice?' Brumbee asked. 'But you've never had an apprentice before.'

Nevery scowled. 'Well, I've got one now. Can you take him?'

Brumbee spared me a quick glance, then looked again, more carefully. 'Yes. Yes, I think so.'

'Good,' Nevery said. He looked down at me. 'Behave yourself, boy, and see if you can learn a thing or two.' He turned to leave.

Brumbee reached out and grabbed his sleeve as he turned away. 'Nevery!'

'What?'

'It's just . . .' The fat wizard lowered his voice. 'We need you here. Thank you for returning to Wellmet.'

At that, Nevery looked surprised. Then he

grasped Brumbee's pudgy hand and gave it a brisk shake, and strode off down the steps and away.

Brumbee watched him go, then turned to me. 'Well, well. Nevery's apprentice, are you?'

I nodded.

'Come with me, please.'

I followed him into a high-ceilinged, echoing gallery. A double stair led down from a second floor balcony, and the floors were paved with slippery black stone. We crossed the wide hall, reaching a door, which stood open. Brumbee led the way through.

'My chambers,' he said. 'My office is here, and a workshop and study. Very convenient.' He shut the door. 'So we won't be disturbed.'

The room was decorated in a darker yellow than Brumbee's robes, and contained a gleaming, carved wooden desk with a comfortable chair behind it, a few benches and bookshelves against the walls, a dark blue rug spangled with stars on the floor, and a few other chairs. A fat black cat was curled on a chair, and a tabby looked up from its perch on the windowsill. I stood just inside the door, and Brumbee crossed to sit behind his desk.

'Well then,' he said, folding his fat hands and looking at me. 'I believe we have met before. Despite the fact that the embero spell is highly illegal, Nevery used it, I think. You were the cat, were you not?'

Drats. He was going to throw me out for spying on the magisters. I thought about lying to him, but there was no point. I nodded.

'Hmmm.' He pointed at one of the chairs. 'Would you like to sit down?'

The chair looked comfortable, but I felt like staying by the door. I knew – *knew* down in my bones – that I was supposed to be Nevery's apprentice. But I was afraid that Brumbee was going to punish me for spying on the magisters by sending me away or telling me I was too stupid to come to his school.

Brumbee was looking through his desk drawers, pulling out paper and pen and ink. He slipped a metal nib onto a pen. 'What is your name?'

'Conn,' I said. That wasn't my whole name,

my true name, but it was enough to start with.

'All right.' Brumbee dipped his pen in the ink and wrote something down on the paper. Then he looked up at me. 'And your age?'

I didn't actually know the answer to that question. I shrugged.

'Hmmm,' Brumbee said. 'How many years of schooling have you already had?'

I didn't say anything. This was a big mistake. I'd be better off going back to Heartsease and trying to persuade Benet to teach me how to read.

Brumbee put down the pen. 'Are you going to answer my questions, Conn?'

I took a deep breath. Nevery wanted me to do this, so I would do it. 'If I can,' I said.

Brumbee looked at me, where I stood by the door. 'Hmmm.' He nodded. 'I think I understand.' He was silent for a moment, thinking. 'Ah, I've got it,' he said to himself, then spoke to me. 'How did you meet your master?'

Now there was a question I could answer. 'I tried to steal his locus magicalicus.'

Brumbee's eyes widened. 'You did *what*?'

'I did steal it, actually,' I said.

'And it didn't kill you?'

I shook my head and stepped closer to the desk. 'It tried to, after a while, but I stopped it. Nevery thought that was interesting, so after he took the locus stone off me, he made me his apprentice.'

'Really!' Brumbee said.

'Well, not exactly,' I said. I sat down in one of the comfortable chairs. 'He took me on as his servant at first, but then he realized that I was supposed to be his apprentice.'

'My goodness,' Brumbee said. 'And so – let me see if I've got this right, Conn – he needs the academicos to teach you some things so you can get on with being a good apprentice.'

'That's right,' I said. 'Mainly, I need to know how to read.'

'Ah. Yes, I see,' Brumbee said. 'To read. We can, of course, teach you that here.'

I felt a sudden relief. He wasn't going to throw me out, after all. 'Can I start today?' I asked.

'It's a bit late for today. But tomorrow,

certainly,' Brumbee said. 'You understand that most students, both the apprentices and the regular students, start at the academicos when they are quite a bit younger than you are?'

I nodded.

Brumbee spoke to himself, fidgeting with his pen. 'But I don't want to put you with the youngest children, do I?' He shook his head. 'No, I don't think that would work. Hmmm.' He fell silent. Then he asked me, 'What have you learned already, Conn?'

'A little bit about locus stones. And not to mix tourmalifine and slowsilver.' I thought back over the past few days. 'And the embero spell, and all the key words for the gates leading to Heartsease, and a spell for making light.'

'Good!' Brumbee said, smiling. 'Would you mind showing me your locus magicalicus?'

Oh. 'I don't have one yet,' I said.

Brumbee stopped smiling. 'Of course you do. You must. Or Nevery would not have taken you on as an apprentice.'

'Well,' I said, 'he did.'

'This is most irregular,' Brumbee said. 'Without a locus stone, how does Nevery—' He cut himself off. 'I shall speak to him about it. He'll have to help you find a locus stone – we have quite a large collection at the academicos; they tend to gather here. And he'll have to present you at Magisters Hall. It is traditional for any wizard's apprentice to be recognized by our governing body.'

I nodded. I'd seen the magisters at work; I wasn't afraid of them.

'As for the reading,' Brumbee went on, 'I think it would be best if you join a class of older students and receive tutoring on the side. You'll have to work very hard to catch up.'

That was all right. I would work hard, and I would catch up.

Frustrated by meeting with magisters.

They had received my letter and would have spent next few weeks discussing my choice of paper and ink if I hadn't arrived when I did.

Fools.

Yet in the end, despite Pettivox's protests, magisters agreed I should lead them through crisis.

Note to self: Send Benet to Sark Square for slowsilver. Must ask Brumbee if magisters have any to spare. Never known it to be so hard to come by.

CHAPTER 13

The next day, Nevery told me I would be presented to the magisters so they could approve me as his apprentice. Then I'd be able to start school.

On our way to Magisters Hall, Nevery seemed distracted. He walked fast through the tunnels, and I had to run to keep up with him. I knew better than to ask him any of the questions bubbling around in my head. What were the magisters going to ask me? Did they know I'd spied on their meetings? Would they care that I couldn't read yet? Would they want to know about my locus magicalicus? Could they tell if I lied to them?

What if they wouldn't accept me?

We arrived at Magisters Hall, and I followed Nevery down a long, echoing hallway. When we got to the big double doors at the end, he said, 'Wait out here, boy, until you're called for.'

Before I could answer, he'd already swept into the magisters' chamber, slamming the door behind him.

I shouldn't have been so nervous. But I was shivery with it. I jittered before the door for a while, waiting for it to open and one of the magisters to drag me in for a wrangle. But no one came. I sat down on the floor to wait.

Finally, the door creaked open and I jumped to

my feet. The wizard named Periwinkle stood in the doorway with her hands on her hips. I peered at her through the ragged fringe of hair hanging in my eyes. She wore the same grey robes as before, with a patch on the sleeve with a blue flower stitched on it, over a plain, dark blue dress; she was broad and strong looking with grey hair in a messy bun.

She looked me up and down. 'You're Nevery's boy?' she asked.

I nodded.

'Well.' She didn't look happy. 'You're not what I expected.'

I wondered what she *had* expected. Somebody taller, maybe.

'Curse Nevery, anyway,' she muttered. 'Boy looks like a gutter rat.'

I looked down at myself. 'But I'm wearing boots,' I said. And my brown coat, a mostly clean shirt, a woollen scarf, and trousers with patches on the knees, not holes.

'Hmmm. Never mind, lad. But tell Nevery to give you a haircut. Now. One thing, before you go in.' She lowered her voice. 'Nevery is not—' She paused and looked at the ceiling, rubbing her chin. 'He is not universally popular among the magisters. Because of that, some of our members may seek to withhold approval of your apprenticeship.'

Politics, she was saying. Some of the magisters might reject me in order to get at Nevery. Even so, I *was* Nevery's apprentice, whether the magisters liked it or not.

She narrowed her eyes. 'Do you understand? Tread carefully, if you can.'

Right, I understood. I nodded.

'Very well.' She turned, pushed the door open wider, and motioned for me to go into the meeting chamber.

The room was as I remembered it, except not as big as it had seemed to the cat me. The table ran the length of the room and had lots of empty seats, as if there had once been more magisters than there were now. On the walls were grimy oil paintings in tarnished frames and a few bookshelves crammed with dusty books that looked like nobody ever read them. At the other end of the room was a wide fireplace with no fire in it.

As I walked into the chamber, the wizards around the table stared at me. They'd been arguing; I could tell by the smoke coming out of Nevery's ears and the snarl on the face of the wizard sitting opposite him at the table.

This had to be Pettivox. He was very tall, taller even than Nevery, and broad, with white hair and beard, gleaming white teeth, and red lips.

And I'd seen him before. He was the wizard I'd seen at the Underlord's, the wizard in the secret underground workroom. I swallowed down my surprise and tried not to stare.

Pettivox wore black wormsilk robes with rows of gold braid at the cuffs and the collar, and a patch on the sleeve with gold-threaded runes stitched on it; he also wore heavy gold rings on his fingers, and had a cloudy white crystal about the size of a thumbnail hanging from a gold chain around his neck. His locus magicalicus. Interesting that he wore it right out in the open like that. Must be proud of it, wanting to show it off.

I didn't like him. He didn't like me, either. He looked at me like you'd look at the bottom of your shoe after you'd stepped in something squishy and smelly.

'Stand over there,' Periwinkle said, pointing to the end of the table. I obeyed, and kept still while the seated wizards inspected me. Nevery gave me a quick glance and looked away, scowling, as if he didn't like what he saw. Periwinkle sat down beside him.

Around the rest of the table sat Brumbee, plump and comfortable in his yellow wormsilk robes; the keen-looking lady, Sandera; the sour, sharp one, Trammel; and, sitting beside Pettivox, the small skinny wizard who looked like a bat, the one who had let the cat me into the chamber before.

Brumbee cleared his throat. 'Ah, Nevery?'

Nevery, still looking furious, gave a curt nod. 'All right, Brumbee, we'll do this according to the forms.' He pointed at me, but glared across the table at Pettivox. 'I, Nevery Flinglas, present to my fellow magisters for their approval this boy, who would be my apprentice.'

'Very good,' Brumbee said quickly, looking nervously around the table. 'This is just a formality, obviously. Can we move to accept Conn as Nevery's apprentice?'

'I reserve the right to pose certain questions,' said Pettivox. Even though he was a big man, his voice was high-pitched and sharp.

Brumbee sighed. 'Of course, Pettivox.'

Of course, I thought. Pose away.

Pettivox leaned forward, vulturelike, his hands folded on the table. 'So. Tell us, Conn, where you lived before coming to your master.'

Hmmm. Not the question I'd been expecting. 'In the Twilight,' I said.

'I see. And you had people looking after you?'

I shook my head. What was he getting at?

Pettivox gave me a false smile. 'Then how did you earn your living in the Twilight?'

I thought about the answer before I gave it. Pettivox was working with Crowe, I guessed, so he might know more about me than he should. Maybe he wanted me to lie so he could catch me out. 'As a thief, mostly,' I said. 'Sometimes I picked pockets, but I'm better at picking locks.'

The magisters didn't like that answer. Periwinkle frowned, and Brumbee fidgeted with his pen. But they would have liked it even less if I'd lied to them.

Pettivox leaned back in his chair and gave Nevery a triumphant look. 'A thief, Nevery? Only you would dare introduce such a person as an apprentice.'

Nevery folded his arms but did not answer.

Sandera spoke up for the first time, her voice clear. 'Isn't it likely, Pettivox, that this boy has already demonstrated his ability to Nevery, which is why he took him on, and why we should accept him?' She looked kindly at me. 'Will you show us your locus magicalicus?'

Drats. I'd been hoping they wouldn't ask about a locus stone. 'I haven't found one yet,' I said.

Pettivox snorted. 'This is ridiculous.' Brumbee, who already knew that I didn't have a locus magicalicus, shook his head. Periwinkle's frown deepened.

Go on, Nevery, I thought. Set them straight.

But Nevery didn't say anything. He sat with

arms crossed, scowling down at the tabletop.

Pettivox said, 'Well, Nevery?'

Nevery remained silent. I shivered and clenched my hands to keep myself still. He was going to change his mind about me.

Finally, he looked up and nodded, as if coming to a decision. 'I do accept him. And you will have to accept him, too, on my word. Or deal with the consequences.'

Pettivox slammed his fist onto the table. 'A threat! Typical! What can Nevery possibly achieve by forcing us to accept as an apprentice a boy thief who has no locus magicalicus and is probably reporting everything he learns to the Underlord.'

'Oh, I don't think so,' Brumbee said hurriedly. 'Conn is not a spy, I don't think.' He shot me a quick glance. 'Not for the Underlord, at any rate. I think we ought to give him a chance, for his own sake, and not just because Nevery asks us to. I propose that we accept him as an apprentice—'

Pettivox opened his mouth to protest, but Brumbee went on quickly, 'Conditionally. If he can find a locus magicalicus in, shall we say, thirty days? Is that enough time, Nevery?'

Nevery nodded. 'It will have to be.' He pointed to the door. 'We're finished with you, boy. Wait outside.'

He didn't have to ask me twice. I skiffed out to wait in the hallway.

I closed the door behind me and leaned against it because my knees were shaking. It hadn't gone too badly, had it? The magisters had accepted me, sort of. I just had to find my locus magicalicus. I had thirty days. But where was I going to start?

CHAPTER 14

After the meeting with the magisters, Nevery and I walked home to Heartsease through the tunnels. I kept quiet, having a lot to think about. Thirty days should be long enough to find a locus magicalicus, shouldn't it? And what about Pettivox? He was a magister. What was he doing working with Crowe?

'Well, boy,' Nevery

138

said, striding along. 'You have provoked my curiosity. I wonder how you survived the Twilight.'

'I have quick hands,' I said. 'And I was lucky.'

'Hmph,' Nevery said, pausing to open a tunnel gate. 'Maybe so. But that's not all of it. Luck and thievery didn't raise you from a baby. Who did?'

Oh. 'My mother,' I said.

We reached the gate leading to Heartsease. Nevery opened it and went through, and I followed him up the stairs to the courtyard. I stopped at the tree and looked west. In the branches above our heads, the black birds stirred, like leaves in a breeze. The sun had just gone down, and, in the distance, the sky over the Twilight was stained with yellowish streaks. A few dim lights shone, like stars through clouds.

Nevery tapped his cane against the cobblestones. 'Well, boy? Tell me about her.'

And he called *me* nosy! 'Her name was Black Maggie,' I said. 'She had black hair and black eyes, and she taught me how to pick locks.' Maggie had taught me how to calm my breath and make my fingers still and quick, no shaking, and she'd taught me how to lift a purse string from a pocket with a feather's touch.

'She's dead?'

I nodded. Killed dead. Crowe had done it. Not himself, he paid minions to do it, to break Maggie's legs so she couldn't walk and then, after a while, she had died. I wasn't going to mention Crowe to Nevery, though, because I didn't want Nevery putting me and Crowe together in the same thought.

'How long ago?' Nevery asked.

The wind gusted. I hunched into my coat, shivering. 'It was the same summer we had all the rain. And the river flooded and all the docks were washed away, remember?'

'No,' Nevery said. He started across the courtyard to the house, whose warm windows were looking out at us. 'I've been banished from Wellmet for twenty years, boy. But there was an exceptionally wet summer about seven years ago, in all of the Peninsular Duchies. Does that seem about right?'

I thought about it. Seven years ago. And I'd

been old enough to take care of myself when Maggie had been killed. When she had died. I nodded.

But I didn't want to talk any more about my mother. 'Nevery?' I asked.

'What,' he said over his shoulder.

I ran a few steps to catch up. 'I've seen Pettivox before.'

'Have you? Where?'

'At the Underlord's.'

We reached the door to the storeroom, and Nevery stood on the step, looking down at me. 'Explain yourself.'

'I had a look 'round while you were talking to the Underlord,' I said.

'Your cursed nosiness will get you into trouble, boy, if you're not careful,' Nevery said.

Probably. 'I think Pettivox is working for the Underlord,' I said.

Nevery scowled. 'And Pettivox happens to be the magister most set against you becoming my apprentice.'

'That's not it, Nevery,' I said.

Nevery turned away, crossed the dark

storeroom, and headed up the narrow stairs. 'Listen, boy,' he said, removing his broad-brimmed hat. 'I suspect Pettivox of many things but not of colluding with the Underlord. He is a magister; it is not in his interest. If you did, in fact, see Pettivox there, which I doubt, it was because he was consulting with the Underlord about the decay of magic in Wellmet. He is as concerned with the loss of magic as any of the magisters are. Now, do not speak of this again.'

All right. I wouldn't.

CHAPTER 15

The next day, Nevery was in a hurry to get to Magisters Hall. He had called a meeting with the Underlord, he said.

'You're asking the wrong person for help,' I said.

'Stay out of it, boy,' Nevery said, sweeping along the tunnel to the academicos. 'You have other things to worry about. I can't help you look for a locus magicalicus. You'll have to find it yourself.'

I had thirty days. Twenty-nine, now. Plenty of time. Still, I wasn't sure, exactly, how I was supposed to find my locus stone. Would it just appear one day? Would I bump my foot on it and just *know* that it was mine? Would it come to me, or would I have to go out into the world to find it?

When we arrived at the academicos, Nevery stopped at the top of the staircase. A student was there, waiting.

'Greetings, Magister Nevery,' she said with a bow. 'Magister Brumbee sent me to meet you here, sir. He said you have an apprentice who needs tutoring?'

He nodded. 'This boy, here.' He pointed at me.

The girl seemed older than I was – she was taller, anyway, and she had catlike grey eyes and bright red hair cut short like she'd hacked it off with a knife. Right from the start, I didn't like her.

'Very well, sir,' the girl said. To me, she said, 'Follow me.'

'Nevery—' I began. I didn't want to go with her.

'Don't argue, boy,' he said. 'And don't give anybody any trouble.' He glared down at me, then went *tap tap tap* down the stairs, on his way to Magisters Hall.

The girl stood looking down her nose at me. 'Hurry up,' she said, walking quickly across the courtyard, ignoring the other students, who stared at me. Following her, I stared back at them. Like the girl, they all wore grey robes over their regular clothes, but they had different colour patches on the sleeves; hers was green with yellow letters.

We went inside and down a hallway to a study room. The girl slung her bag onto the floor, sat down on a bench facing me, and leaned back against the table. Beneath her grey robe, she wore an embroidered black wormsilk dress down to her ankles, and black lace-up boots. She took a few moments to look me up and down.

'What's your name?' she asked. 'I suppose you do have one, besides "boy".'

'Conn,' I answered. 'Connwaer.' Now why had I done that? Nobody knew my own true name, only Nevery. And I'd gone and told this horrible girl.

'Connwaer,' she said, looking up at the ceiling. 'It's a kind of bird, isn't it?'

Yes, and she'd better not say anything more about it.

'Black feathers?'

I nodded.

She gave me a glinting look, all sly and sharp. 'Suits you.'

I blinked, surprised. Maybe she wasn't so bad, after all.

'I'm Rowan. I'm a regular student, not a wizard's apprentice, but I sit in on the apprentice classes. Magister Brumbee told me you need to learn how to read.'

'That's right,' I said.

She bent to pull some things out of her bag: paper, pencils, a couple of books. 'I've never taught anybody to read before. I have no idea why Magister Brumbee gave me this assignment.' She waved me over.

I went and sat next to her on the bench. 'Maybe he's mad at you,' I said.

'Hah,' she said, and gave me the glinting look

again. 'I think he wants to teach me patience.'

She seemed like an impatient person; that might be the reason.

Rowan opened one of the books, which had big runes written across the pages. 'This is a rune book, obviously, from the babies' class.' She quickly told me the names of the runes, then shoved the book along the table to me. 'There. Look at them for a while yourself. I've got some studying of my own to do.' She opened the other book.

I flipped the pages back and looked at the runes again, then paged forward until I came to the words. If I put the runes together, they made patterns – words. I worked at that for a while, until Rowan closed her book and pulled my book away from me.

'All right, that's enough,' she said. 'I'm going to drill you on your runes.'

'What d'you mean?' I asked.

She blew out a sigh. 'I'm going to test you, to see if you know which runes are which.'

I didn't get it. 'But I already know that.'

She put her elbow on the table and her chin

on her hand and looked at me. 'You learned the runes?'

'And how to put them together to make words.'

'Right. Show me.'

I took the book back from her and put together some of the words.

She gave me the down-the-nose look she'd given me before. 'So you *did* know how to read before.'

'No, I didn't,' I said.

She shook her head. 'You're lying.'

'Why would I lie about something like that?' I asked. I could think of much better things to lie about.

She stared at me for a while. 'I guess you wouldn't. But you learned that awfully fast.' She gave a sudden, bright smile, which made her sharp, proud face look much friendlier. 'Maybe I'm just a really good teacher.'

At that moment, the door flew open and a group of grey-robed students burst into the room. Rowan's face went back to looking proud and sharp, and she snapped the rune book closed.

'Oh, sorry, Lady Rowan,' one of the students said, breathlessly. 'We didn't know you were studying in here.' They started to back out.

Rowan shoved the papers and her book back into her bag. 'No, it's all right,' she told the students. 'We're all finished.' She gave me the rune book. 'Here. Study this tonight, and we'll go on with your lessons tomorrow.'

As she got to her feet, I noticed the patch on her sleeve. In the middle was a slender tree, stitched with green and yellow thread. Below it was a line of things that I now knew were runes. They made words. Rowan's patch said *T-R-E-E* and *L-E-A-F*.

Underlord came to Magisters Hall, rowed across river with three bodyguards. Underlord not a big man, speaks quietly, but fills room with his presence. Powerful.

Underlord very calm. —I share your concern, Magister Nevery, he said.

Doubted it. Not a wizard, how could he?

—I realize I have a bad reputation east of the river, Crowe said. He put his hand into his pocket, followed by odd clicking noise. —But Magister Nevery, I am just a businessman trying in hard times to keep the factories open so the workers can earn their wages.

Very likely this true. Why would Crowe work to reduce the level of magic in city if it meant factories would no longer operate? Makes no sense.

—At the same time, Crowe said, —my calculations indicate that the crisis has been exaggerated.

—Why so, I asked.

Underlord shrugged, very smooth. Then sound of odd clicking noise again. —The werelights in the Sunrise still light that part of the city. The factories are running.

They run thirty per cent slower, but they are running.
I see no reason for panic.

Underlord folded his hands on the table and leaned
forward. —What, precisely, are the magisters doing to
remedy the problem? he asked.

—We are studying the situation, I said. —And
have little to report.

This actually true, unfortunately.

After more pointless discussion, Crowe left.

Hadn't met this Underlord before return to Wellmet.
Crowe civilized man. Still, not to be trusted.

CHAPTER 16

I spent six days going to school with Rowan, while keeping an eye open for my locus magicalicus. The reading was going well. The searching was not.

On the seventh day, Rowan met me at the

academicos steps. She had her book bag with her and looked impatient.

'You're late, Conn,' she said, turning to lead the way into the main entry, the two-storey gallery with the staircases and shiny stone floor. 'No lesson today.' She paused and pointed toward Brumbee's door. 'The magister wants to talk to you.' She shot me her glinting look. 'You in trouble, young man?'

I hoped not.

'Well,' she said, 'good luck.'

Thanks. I nodded at her and crossed the hall to knock on Brumbee's door.

'Come in!' his voice called. I opened the door and edged inside. 'Ah, Conn,' Brumbee said. He sat behind his desk, which was piled with papers and books bristling with page markers. He waved at one of the comfortable chairs before his desk; his two cats sat in the other one. 'I'm not due at Magisters Hall for half an hour. That should give us a little time.'

Good. I needed to talk to somebody about my locus stone problem. I went over to the chair and sat down.

'How are the lessons with your tutor?' Brumbee asked.

'All right,' I answered.

'Are you learning your runes?'

I nodded. I didn't really want to talk to Brumbee about schooling. And I could tell he didn't want to talk about anything but my schooling.

'Good!' He beamed.

'Brumbee,' I said, before he could ask me if I'd learned to spell C-O-N-N. 'How do I find my locus magicalicus?'

'Ah.' He shifted in his chair, then opened a drawer of his desk, as if looking for something. 'Well, you know, Conn, that is for Nevery to help you with.'

'He doesn't have time,' I said.

'Yes,' Brumbee said unhappily. 'I know. This situation with the magical decay. It's a very serious problem, and we are relying on Nevery to figure out what's going on.'

I nodded. I knew it was serious. Nevery had been very distracted, spending hours tinkering with devices and magical calibrations in his workroom, or staying up all night to pore over books, searching for precedents to the situation in Wellmet, or meeting with the other magisters. From the looks of it, he hadn't found any answers, and he was frustrated and short-tempered as a result.

'It's awkward, Conn. Do you understand?'

I didn't, really.

Brumbee went on, fidgeting with a pen he'd taken from a drawer. 'The thing is, my boy, it's very odd that Nevery has taken you on before you've found your locus stone.'

A sinking feeling gathered in my stomach. He didn't think I should be an apprentice. 'I *am* a wizard, Brumbee,' I said. 'And I only have twenty-three days left to find my locus magicalicus,' I said.

Brumbee sighed and nodded. 'And Nevery is too busy. Very well, then. I will help you, Conn, as much as I am able.'

I took a deep breath of relief.

Brumbee stood and bustled toward the door. 'Come with me. We'll start with our collection here and see what happens.'

He led me into a dark, dusty back room of the library. 'Ah, here we are. Let me just fetch us a light.'

I waited in the darkness until he returned carrying a stand with six candles on it. He pulled out his locus magicalicus, which was round and brown, like an egg. He used it to light the candles, whispering a word and touching the stone to each wick, which sputtered and then blossomed into light.

As the room brightened, I saw that it was full of wooden boxes, all labelled and stacked neatly on shelves.

'Yes, very good. In these boxes,' Brumbee said, pointing at the shelves, 'are locus magicalicus stones, carefully catalogued. They wash up here at the academicos, and we collect them and wait for their wizards to turn up. Sometimes they do and sometimes they don't; we have lots of stones and not many wizards, you see. We keep the stones, just in case.'

I nodded. But I reckoned people from the Twilight didn't show up often to claim a stone.

'Here's what you must do,' Brumbee went on.

'Go through the boxes carefully. Touch each stone but be sure to put it back just where you found it. If your locus magicalicus is here, it will call to you.'

Right. 'What does the call sound like?'

Brumbee pursed his lips. 'It is different for every wizard. For some, the call can be nearly undetectable, like a whisper. For others, it is a kind of tingling connection. In some rare cases, I'm told, the call of the locus stone is overwhelming, like being caught up in a gigantic wave of magic.' He shook his head. 'At any rate, if your stone is here, you will know it is yours when you touch it.' He smiled and patted me on the shoulder. 'Now, I must go to Magisters Hall. I will leave you to it, shall I?'

'Thank you,' I said.

'You're welcome, my lad,' Brumbee said. 'Best luck.' He went out, and the candle flames jumped in the breeze from the door closing as he left.

I looked at the boxes, tidy, labelled rows of them, piled from floor to ceiling. Going methodically through them would take days.

And my locus magicalicus was not here, I knew it already.

Too much to do. Device construction going very slowly. Can't get cursed verity crystals properly aligned. Hardly a drop of slowsilver to be found in city. And spent fifteen hours in academicos library, still have thousands of pages to read, notes to transcribe, collate.

Need secretary. Absolutely certain boy hasn't temperament for secretarial work. Asks too many questions. And his handwriting is terrible. Will ask Brumbee for advanced student at academicos to assist me.

Left library late, close to midnight. Walking through tunnel toward Heartsease, came to locked gate. Boy curled up in corner shadows, asleep.

Had forgotten about him. Cursed nuisance. Nudged him with foot to wake him up.

Pulled out my locus magicalicus, said the opening words. —Well, boy, I said. —You've been waiting all this time. Why didn't you just pick the lock to get through?

He stood up stiffly, followed me through gate when it opened. —I tried to, he said.

Imagine the lock singed his thieving fingers for him.

Walked through tunnels to Heartsease without speaking further. Went up to kitchen. Benet asleep, so told boy to make tea while I warmed my fingers before the fire. Cursed academicos library cold and damp has gotten into my bones.

Note to self: Must get Benet stove for cooking.

Boy brought cup of tea and a biscuit. Very quiet.

Come to think of it, boy often quiet. Not a chatterer. Fortunate because will not tolerate chattering. Drank tea, warmed up.

—Well, boy, I said. —You are a master lockpick, are you?

Boy nodded.

Finished tea, went up to study, where I keep several locked boxes. There, boy taught me to pick locks. Not as easy as one might think.

Some of boy's instruction:

Keys have flanges.

Trick is to insert wires into lock to replace flanges.

Easy to do when key has just one flange; wire turns lock like a bolt and, as boy says, YOU'RE IN.

Some keys have flanges all around barrel. These, boy says, are TRICKY.

160

Other keys have crenellations or studs, and some have flanges, studs, and crenellations, and these, boy says, are REALLY INTERESTING.

Locks are like puzzles, according to boy. But good lockpick can open even trickiest puzzle lock in under a minute.

Boy also advises that lockpick should carry at least two sets of wires, and one should be hidden in case he's taken up by city guards. Picked up one of Benet's knitting needles from table, said it could be useful to lockpick. Says a little knife is good to have as well, because a lockpick with, as he calls it, QUICK HANDS, can use it to pick easy locks.

Don't believe there is any such thing as EASY LOCK.

Giving it a try, managed to lock myself out of study, boy inside warming himself by fire. Wouldn't let me in, curse him. Finally picked lock, got in.

Expect picking pockets more difficult skill to learn.

CHAPTER 17

Twenty days left.

I hadn't bothered going through the academicos collection of locus stones. As a result, Brumbee was disappointed in me.

'My locus magicalicus isn't in there,' I said.

'But how can you be sure?' Brumbee said. 'You haven't looked carefully.'

'It just isn't.'

He shook his head and sent me away. He couldn't, he said sadly, spare me any more attention if I wasn't going to make an effort.

Eighteen days.

Rowan had told her teachers that I was ready to join the other students in the apprentice class. For some reason, she was in the class, too.

'Ordinarily,' she'd explained, 'regular students don't need to know much about magic. But I'm interested.'

'Even though you're not an apprentice?' I'd asked.

'Even though, Connwaer.'

But Rowan wasn't always in class. When she wasn't, I missed her.

The apprentice class was held in a long room with a high ceiling and lots of windows to let in plenty of light. Dust floated in the air, sparkling like tiny stars in the beams of weak winter sunlight.

Only five students, plus me, were in the class, and that day we sat in three groups of two, passing a spelltext back and forth, reading the spell out loud in quiet voices. The words must roll smoothly from the tongue, Periwinkle told us – she was our teacher – without hesitation or error, in order to invoke the magic.

Because I was the worst student, Periwinkle had put me with the best student. Keeston was a bigger boy who was very proud of his locus stone, which was shiny black like Nevery's, but splintery looking. The patch on his robe had a stone arch embroidered on it. He was also proud of his looks; he was tall and strong, and had wavy fair hair and dark blue eyes. He was Pettivox's apprentice, and he was proud of that, too.

He wasn't happy about working with me. I still couldn't read very well out loud. I was slowing him down, he said. Keeston sneered every time I had to stop and put the runes together to make words.

And then we came to a spell I knew something about. The embero, the spell Nevery had used to turn me into a cat. Keeston had the book, and was reading the embero spell out loud. Then he made a mistake.

'It's *tark*olil,' I said, interrupting him.

Keeston gave me the eyeball. 'It is not, new boy. It's *terk*olil. Says so in the book. Can't you *read*?'

'Yes, I can,' I said. 'The book is wrong. It's *tark*olil.'

Keeston sat back in his seat and gave me a scornful look. 'Magister,' he called.

Periwinkle, her grey hair straggling from its bun, came over. 'You have a question, Keeston?'

'Not really, Magister,' Keeston answered. 'The new boy thinks the embero spell has the word *tarkelel* in it.'

He'd gotten it wrong again. '*Tarkolil*,' I said.

'Look, Magister,' Keeston said, pointing at the book, which lay open on the table. 'The new boy is being stupid about this.'

Periwinkle leaned over to peer at the book. 'Ah, yes.' She cast me a silencing glare and straightened. 'Keeston, you are correct and Conn is in error.'

I stared at her. I knew I was right.

Keeston smirked.

'Now, apprentices,' Periwinkle said to the class. 'You may each open your books again and study the next chapter.' Then she leaned over to speak softly to me. 'And you, Conn, will forget everything you know about the embero, if you know what's good for you.'

'The book is wrong,' I whispered back.

Periwinkle glanced up at the ceiling, blew out a breath, and looked back down again. 'Of course it is. The book is intentionally in error. Our students would have no good reason to use the embero, which is a particularly dangerous spell. So it was written down with a mistake in it, just so students don't effect it by accident and turn themselves into toads.'

Right, I got it. But I didn't have to like it. 'That's a stupid thing to do with the magic. Why teach them spells they can't use?'

'Hush,' Periwinkle said, pointing at my book. 'Keep quiet and read.'

Frowning, I opened my book and started reading.

Rowan came in late, then, and slid onto a seat beside me. 'What did I miss?' she whispered. She was out of breath.

'Toads,' I said quietly. 'Where've you been?'

She shrugged and opened her spelltext. 'Affairs of state, my lad.'

Ha-ha. I showed her the page we were on and went back to piecing together the larpenti spell, for turning water into other liquids. I wondered where the mistake in the spell was, and if Nevery would teach me the real larpenti spell.

After class was over, I said good-bye to Rowan, slung my bag full of books over my shoulder, and headed for the stairs to the secret tunnels to wait for Nevery. I was thinking about where I was going to look next for my locus magicalicus when Keeston and three of his friends, a boy and two girls, appeared in front of me.

I started to walk around them, but they moved to block my way to the stairs.

'Magister Nevery is your master, is he?' Keeston asked.

Nothing wrong with that question. I nodded.

'But you don't have a locus magicalicus. So you can't be sure you're really a wizard, can you?'

I knew for sure that I was a wizard, but I didn't have to prove it to Keeston. I shrugged.

Keeston stepped closer. '*Can* you?'

'I'll find a locus stone.' Eventually.

Keeston stepped closer. 'My master says he'd have you beaten, sneak thief, if you were his apprentice.'

I put my bag down, to keep my hands free. Only one way this kind of conversation was likely to lead. 'What for, footlicker?' I asked.

'For disrespect, among other things,' Keeston sneered.

That didn't make sense. 'But I respect Nevery.'

'See, right there?' Keeston glanced aside to his three grey-robed friends, and they nodded. He looked back at me. 'You called your master—' He couldn't bring himself to say Nevery's name.

The other apprentices were frightened of Nevery. I saw how they quivered like jelly on a plate whenever he was around. I'd heard them tell stories among themselves; they'd heard them from their masters, I reckoned. Like that twenty years ago Nevery had been banished from Wellmet for attempting to kill the duchess, which I didn't believe, and for trying to burn down the Dawn Palace, which, knowing Nevery, could be true.

At any rate, Keeston was still worked up about it. 'You call your master by his right name,' he said.

I nodded.

'You should call him "Master".'

I nodded again. 'Yes, he told me that, too. But we agreed that if I taught him to pick locks, I could call him Nevery.'

Keeston drew himself up and spoke triumphantly. 'See there?' His friends, lined up like little dolls in a shop window, nodded again. 'Right there. My master would have you beaten for that, gutterboy.'

'Like he beats you, crawler?' I asked.

And then he went for me.

I wasn't expecting it yet, so he got in one punch, right in my face.

Keeston was bigger than I was, but you don't last long in the Twilight without learning how to fight. Shaking off the blow he'd given me, I ducked under his next swing and gave him a sharp elbow under the ribs. As he bent over, gasping for breath, I kicked him in the collops. He fell to the ground, howling.

His friends, if that's what they were, backed away, eyes wide.

Drats. I'd probably get in trouble for this. And my face hurt where Keeston had hit me. Oh well. I heaved up my book bag, walked around them, and headed for the stairs.

That night, before supper, Nevery and I sat in the study, he in his chair at one end of the table, me at the other end with my books and papers. I had a lot of reading to do, and Rowan had insisted that I work on my handwriting, which she said was atrocious.

I got right down to it, putting my elbows on the table, propping my head in my hands, and working through a history book. It was very interesting stuff, about the origins of magic in the Peninsular Duchies, of which Wellmet was one. Each city was part of a loose . . .

I had to stop and take the word apart. *Con-fed-er-acy*. I got up and fetched the lexicon from the bookshelf and brought it back to my place at the table. Looked up the word. *Confederacy: An alliance of different groups or people for a common purpose.* What was that purpose, I wondered. I kept reading to see if I could find out.

Wellmet, the text went on, was one of a loose confederacy of cities, each built on a magical node. A magical node, the lexicon said, was a place where, for some reason yet to be determined, magic gathered. Between the nodes, in places where there was little or no magic, were vast wildernesses and deserts and, closer to the cities, farmland, mines, and forests.

I'd never thought about any of these things before. Before coming to Nevery, I'd never really thought about anything beyond finding enough to eat and a warm place to sleep. It was fascinating. Magic was the life of a place, and attracted people, so the cities grew up on magical nodes. It made perfect sense.

'—*Are* you listening, boy?' Nevery asked loudly.

I looked up, blinking. What?

He pointed at my face. 'You've been fighting again, have you? Benet?'

Oh. I felt the place where Keeston had hit me. A bruise, probably nice and purple by now, under my eye. 'No,' I answered. 'Keeston. A boy at the academicos.'

'Hmmm,' Nevery said. 'Pettivox's apprentice, I think.'

I nodded.

He gave me a stern look. 'I won't tolerate fighting, boy.'

'I know. But I don't like him.'

Nevery raised his eyebrows. 'Really.'

'Really,' I answered. 'Look, Nevery, it doesn't bother me that Keeston calls me gutterboy and sneak thief, because that's what I am. But he jumped on me when I called him what he is.'

'Indeed.' Nevery leaned back in his chair and pulled on the end of his beard. 'And what is that?'

'Footlicker and crawler.'

'Ah.' He looked at me, lips twitching. 'And he blacked your eye for you.'

Yes, he had.

'Well, boy. Don't let it happen again.'

Typical Nevery comment. Did he mean don't let Keeston black my eye again? Don't fight with him again? Don't let him call me gutterboy again? Don't call him crawler again?

I bent my head over my book, but I couldn't concentrate. I kept going over the fight – and it hadn't been much of a fight, really – and thinking about what Keeston had said and why he had said it. Hmmm. Maybe Keeston hadn't jumped me because I called him a crawler, but because . . .

'Nevery?' I said.

He looked up from his book. 'What, boy?'

I thought about it for a moment. 'I think Keeston's master beats him.'

Nevery studied me. 'Are you worried that I'd have you beaten for something?'

The thought hadn't even occurred to me. I considered it. 'No.'

'You wouldn't stand for it, would you,' Nevery said.

Not even from Nevery, no. I shook my head.

Nevery nodded. 'That is why you, boy, are not a gutterboy or sneak thief.'

Ah. That made perfect sense. Still, I decided, I'd keep my eye on Keeston. I wasn't so sure he was a bad sort. I'd likely jump on people, too, if I had a master who beat me.

Of course, if I didn't find my locus magicalicus soon, I wouldn't be an apprentice anymore. I wasn't sure what I'd be. Nothing, maybe.

At dinner, after evening of studying, boy asked about nature of magic.

Question every apprentice asks, eventually.

Explained Micnu's theory on magical emergence. —Micnu wrote a treatise explaining that magic most likely emerges from some kind of geological and atmospheric convergence.

—Atmospheric convergence, boy repeated slowly.

Explained further. —GEOLOGICAL, having something to do with the way the ground below our feet behaves, and ATMOSPHERIC, having to do with the air above, including the weather. You need to read more widely, I said.

—I don't have time, boy said.

—Make the time, boy. Now, Micnu's theories are widely accepted, but they are not the only ideas about the nature of magic. Carron's writings, which are over five hundred years old, argue that magic underlies the land as water does and wells up in some places.

Boy nodded. —What would Micnu and Carron say about the magic leaving Wellmet?

A good question. —What do you think? I asked.

Boy thought for few minutes. Benet served out fish and stewed greens, passed biscuits around. I ate and waited.

—Right, boy said. —I figure Micnu would say there's been a change in Wellmet's weather or maybe an earthquake, and that's changed the con . . . the convergence. And Carron would say that the well is running dry.

I nodded. Essentially, this correct.

—But, Nevery, boy said. —I don't think that's it.

Benet, adding more biscuits to basket, snorted.

—Well, boy, I said. —What is it, then?

—I don't know, boy said. He took a bit of fish from his plate, fed it to his cat, under table. Sat up, said, —I need to think about it some more.

Need to think about it, too. Interesting conversation. Tend to agree that neither Micnu or Carron's ideas explain what is happening to Wellmet. After dinner, took boy to study, gave him first book in Carron's annals and Micnu's treatise to read.

Meet tomorrow with advanced student from academicos; someone likely to have skills to assist me.

CHAPTER 18

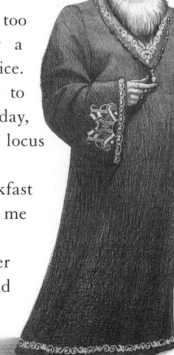

Sixteen days left. I'd been wasting too much time being a student and an apprentice. From now on, I needed to spend all day, every day, searching for my locus magicalicus.

We were eating breakfast at the table in the kitchen, me and Nevery and Benet.

'Nevery,' I said, after taking a bite of porridge and

wiping my mouth.

'Use your napkin, boy, not your sleeve,' Nevery growled.

I looked at my sleeve. What did he mean?

Nevery held up his napkin, then used it to wipe his mouth.

Oh, that's what it was for. I used my napkin and then went back to my question. 'Nevery, I need one of those password stones for the tunnel gates.'

'You need a haircut, is what you need,' Benet said.

I didn't have time for haircuts. 'Can I have one, Nevery?'

'A keystone?' Nevery said, taking a drink and setting down his teacup. 'Why, boy?'

The bite of porridge I was eating turned to ashes in my mouth. I swallowed it down. 'I need to go out into Wellmet and search for my locus magicalicus,' I said.

'Yes, all right.' He pointed at me with his spoon. 'But you go to the academicos every day.'

I didn't answer. I wasn't going to go to school. I didn't have time.

I was from the Twilight. So, I reckoned, I'd find my locus magicalicus in the Twilight.

And if I was going to search in the Twilight, I had to look like I belonged there. If I went in wearing my coat and hat and woollen scarf, and my stout boots, somebody – some thief or bagman – would jump on me, drag me into an alley, and pluck me like a chicken.

So after stepping onto the west side of the river, I found the nearest alley, where I took off my warm clothes and boots and hid them in a dry hole under a flat stone, and rubbed dirt on my face and in my hair and on my bare feet. Takes a while to work up a really good layer of grime, but it would do.

Then I went out and searched.

I started down by the river, sticking to the shadows in the warehouse district, slinking past the docks and the dockside taverns. Nothing. Farther south, the docks ended and mudflats lined the river. When I'd lived in the Twilight I'd gone mudlarking, because you could find, washed up in the mud, metal to sell, and sometimes a copper lock or two on a rotting purse string, or a bundle of old clothes.

Mudlarking for my locus magicalicus was hopeless. All I got for my trouble was cold. And muddy.

Ten days.

I moved on from the riverside and tried the workers' tenements in the Steeps, but found nothing. Then I tried the area around Dusk House, the Underlord's mansion.

Late in the afternoon, I was searching in an alleyway, digging through a pile of garbage – rags and rotting wood, broken bottles and a dead rat – when I looked up and saw a man in a black wizard's robe stride past the mouth of the alley. Pettivox!

If he was going to see the Underlord again, he was up to something, sure as sure, no matter what Nevery said.

I edged out of the alley. As he climbed the street, I followed, keeping to the shadows.

He veered off, cutting down a side street, toward the river, then down a steep set of stairs until he came out at one of the factories along the river. I lurked in a doorway until he went inside.

Tricky following him in there. But I had to find out what Pettivox was up to.

The factory was a huge building built of soot-stained brick, with belching chimneys and narrow windows painted black. I slid in the doorway, not far behind the wizard, glad it was dark and dusty. And noisy with the clatter-rattle of millworks; it was a factory for making cloth. Workers, coming and going past whirring machines for spinning thread, looked like sooty black ghosts. At the machines themselves, powered by magic brought in through huge, pulsing pipes overhead, rows of children bent their heads, threading spindles with quick fingers. Their hair was shaved short so it wouldn't be caught in the machines and yanked off their heads. They didn't even look up as I passed.

Pettivox stood at the end of a row of whirling bobbins. Another man, a factory boss dressed in a black suit, spoke with him. They shouted to be heard above the rattling machines, so, even lurking deep in the shadows, I heard most of what they said.

'Can you get some more?' Pettivox shouted.

The factory man shook his head and muttered something.

Pettivox scowled. '. . . must have more slow-silver! If you don't get it, the Underlord will—' He leaned over and snarled something right into the other man's face; the man flinched away. Then he nodded.

At that, Pettivox whirled away and stalked down the dim-dark millwork rows, and I followed him out into the day, which, grey as it was, seemed bright after the factory.

Pettivox headed up the steep street again, me not far behind him. He turned a corner – still headed toward the Underlord's – and I hurried to catch up, but he was striding along quickly.

Too far ahead, he turned another corner. I raced up the street and pelted around the corner into an alley, and he was there, waiting.

'Hah!' he said, and grabbed me. His eyes narrowed as he realized who I was. 'You!'

Still gripping me by the arms, Pettivox shoved me deeper into the alley; I looked over my shoulder and saw, behind me, that the narrow alley led to a brick wall. Dead end. Trapped.

'Nevery's boy,' Pettivox said. I twisted out of his grip and backed up a step, trying to catch my breath. He stepped after me, forcing me deeper into the alley. 'You were following me,' he said. 'You're poking your nose in where it doesn't belong, thief. You should be careful a blackbird doesn't come along and snip it off.'

Underlord Crowe, he meant.

Pettivox gave me a nasty smile, his white teeth gleaming. 'What would Nevery think if his little spy went missing? I wonder.'

He'd think I'd run away, was what he would think. I couldn't let Pettivox drag me in to see the Underlord, because I'd never get away again.

As he reached out to grab me, I ducked under his hands and dived to the ground, rolling out of the alley. He turned, shouting something, but I was already on my feet, racing down the cobbled street. He didn't follow, but I kept running, around corners, down steep alley steps, until my breath was tearing at my lungs and my legs felt quivery and weak.

Finally I reached the alley where I'd hidden my coat and boots. Gasping for breath, I leaned against the brick wall. Stupid, almost getting caught like that. Stupid. I'd have to be more careful.

'Any luck?' Nevery asked when I brought him tea late that night.

I shook my head. 'Nevery, I saw Pettivox in the Twilight.'

'Not now, boy,' Nevery said. 'And you didn't put any honey in the tea.'

Without saying anything, I took the tea down to the kitchen, put honey in, and brought it back up. Nevery said an absentminded thank-you, his nose deep in a fat book, some long-dead wizard's grimoire he'd borrowed from the academicos library. Clear as clear, he didn't want to be bothered with anything else. I left quietly and went up to my attic room. By the light of a candle, I read Micnu's treatise. When it got late enough, I blew out the light and wrapped my blankets around me. But I couldn't sleep.

Nine days. Eight. Seven. Six . . .

I spent all day, every day, wandering through the cold, damp streets of the Twilight, searching for my locus magicalicus. I hoped that I'd be walking along and I'd accidentally kick a rock and a tingle of recognition would run through me, and I'd feel compelled to pick up the stone, and it would be mine – my locus stone, proof that I was a wizard, my reason for staying at Heartsease with Nevery.

But as the days passed, I got nothing except bruised toes.

Five days.

I came back late to Heartsease, dirty, cold, and hungry, slinking from the secret tunnel and across the dark courtyard, trying not to wake the birds in the black tree. I didn't want to hear them scold. The mansion stood tall, a ragged shadow against the night, except for the warm golden glow of the windows.

I went inside and climbed wearily up to the

kitchen, tired down to my bones. Benet was there. His knitting, a snarl of black yarn, sat on the table. Nevery had gotten him a stove, so he was busy setting it up, angling the stovepipe so it would carry the smoke out a window. He'd knocked out a pane and stood on a chair, trying to plug the gaps between the window frame and the pipe so the cold air couldn't come in. Lady sat watching him, her tail curled over her paws, and a bright fire burned in the hearth.

Benet glanced at me as I came in. 'Anything?' he asked.

I shook my head.

'Huh,' he grunted, and turned back to the window.

I sat down, folded my arms on the table, and put my head down to rest, just for a moment.

I woke up with a crick in my neck and Benet poking my arm. He pointed at the ceiling. 'Tea.'

Right. I sat up and rubbed my eyes. It was late. Nevery would be wanting tea.

Benet handed me the tray. There were two cups on it, a teapot, and a plate of bread and butter. I looked blankly at it. 'He's not going to have time to drink tea with me, Benet,' I said.

'It's not for you,' Benet said gruffly.

Not for me. Who, then?

'He's taken on a secretary,' Benet said. 'Student from the academicos. To help him with the reading and writing.'

A secretary, right.

I trudged up the stairs to the study and went in with the tea tray. Nevery was there with his new secretary.

Keeston.

I stopped inside the door, frozen. Keeston and Nevery were sitting at the table surrounded by books and papers. A fire burned in the hearth. Very companionable and cosy.

Keeston looked up from his work and gave me a nasty smile. 'Your servant has brought tea, Magister Nevery,' he said.

I thawed out enough to go in and carefully pushed aside a few books to put the tray on the table. 'I'm not his servant.' Crawler toady.

Nevery looked up. I didn't expect him to add anything, but he did. 'He is my apprentice, Keeston.'

'Yes, of course, Magister,' Keeston said quickly, turning a little pale.

I turned to leave.

'Wait, boy,' Nevery said. I turned back. He pointed at Keeston. 'Go down and tell Benet we'll need more tea later. It's going to be a late night.'

'Yes, Magister,' Keeston said, scrambling to his feet and hurrying from the room.

As the door closed behind him, Nevery turned his gaze on me. 'Well?'

'He's Pettivox's,' I said. And I was certain, now that I'd seen him again in the Twilight, where he had no business going, that Pettivox was working for the Underlord.

'We've spoken of this before, boy. Pettivox is a magister, as I am, and he has done well to offer me his apprentice's services.' Nevery scowled. 'We are working together to solve the crisis facing the city.'

'The Underlord has something to do with it,' I said.

Nevery gave me an exasperated look. 'This has nothing to do with Underlord Crowe.'

I had a feeling that it did have something to do with Crowe, and with his underground workshop, and with Pettivox. But Nevery didn't want to hear about it. And I was too tired to argue. Couldn't seem to think straight about anything.

'Now, boy,' he said, pointing at the door. 'You're obviously exhausted. Go to bed.'

To bed, right. I stumbled toward the door. Paused. 'Just be careful what you tell Keeston.'

'I am not a fool, boy,' Nevery said. 'Keeston is useful to me.'

And I was not, he was saying. Drats.

I went to bed.

Four days left.

Still nothing.

I decided to stop off at the academicos to see if Brumbee had some maps of the city. I was just about finished with the Twilight and was going to have to face crossing the river to search the Sunrise, the duchess's part of the city.

I used the keystone to pass through the tunnel gates. The air was cold and damp, the walls dripping with slime, the floors covered with a shallow film of water. Slippery. Like being on the inside of a snake.

As I reached the academicos gate, I saw a dark, hunched figure; somebody was sitting on the bottom step of the stairs leading up.

Rowan. She got stiffly to her feet, arms folded, looking impatient. 'What are you up to, young Connwaer?'

I wondered how long she'd been sitting there. A while, maybe; she looked cold. 'Hello, Rowan.'

'Yes, hello and all that,' she said crossly. 'I've waited for you every morning, and you never come. You've stopped coming to school, have you?'

I nodded. 'I need to talk to Brumbee.'

'About coming back to the academicos?'

'No,' I said, stepping around her. 'About finding my locus stone.'

She stepped to the side, blocking me. 'Yes, Magister Brumbee told me about that. And you're almost out of time, are you?'

Hearing her saying it out loud like that made my stomach leap up and wrestle with my throat for a minute.

I must have turned pale, because she went on, hurriedly, 'Surely it's not more important than going to school.'

'It is,' I said.

She put her hands on her hips and glared. 'You're being stupid, Conn. You'll find your locus magicalicus eventually. Until you do, just work for Magister Nevery.'

'I can't.'

'Why not? It seems the obvious solution.'

I just couldn't do it. I shook my head.

'Very well,' Rowan said. In the dim light, her red hair looked like a banked fire and her eyes flashed with annoyance. She spun on her heel and stalked away, up the stairs.

Have found precedent for city's loss of magic. Secretary came across crumbling old text in academicos library. Account of destruction of Arhionvar, lost city of the Fierce Mountains.

According to text, Arhionvar was thriving crossroads of trade on potent magical node, when suddenly, magic drained from city. Without lifeblood of magic, Arhionvar died. Text speculates that death of Arhionvar not a natural phenomenon. Troubling.

Have not yet felt sense of urgency, but suspect we should be more alarmed. Possible boy's ideas have some merit: loss of magic in Wellmet could be human-caused problem. Wouldn't blame Underlord for such a thing, as boy is so quick to do, because Crowe is not a wizard, and because Crowe would not benefit if magic were lost. But must think further on it.

Secretary proving useful. Organized. Neat handwriting. Follows orders. Doesn't plague me with questions.

CHAPTER 19

Today was the last day.

In the kitchen, Benet greeted me with a glare. 'Listen, you. Stop messing about,' he growled. 'Find the stone and be done with it.'

I didn't answer, just grabbed the bucket and went out for water. When I got back, I left the bucket by the hearth and went down to fetch more wood for the fire. By that time, Benet had breakfast ready for Nevery and Keeston; two cups, a steaming teapot, and a basket of muffins. He pointed to the stairs, and I took it up. They weren't in the study, so I went up to the workroom. Knocked.

'Breakfast, Nevery,' I said.

After a long moment, he answered, his voice sharp. 'Leave it outside the door, boy, and go away.'

I put down the tray. Then I leaned my forehead against the door. Maybe he'd lost count of the days. Right. He probably didn't remember that this was the last day. I wanted to talk to him before I left. But I couldn't go in there while he and Keeston were working on some experiment that couldn't be interrupted.

I went back downstairs to the kitchen.

Lady was there, purring before the fire. I crouched beside her to get warm before heading out to search. What I really wanted to do was go back to bed. I was tired. I was starting to believe that I wasn't going to find a locus magicalicus. Maybe I wasn't a wizard after all.

'Here, you,' Benet said, interrupting my dark

thoughts. I looked up. He was elbow deep in bread dough; he raised a floury finger to point at the table.

I went over to see. A black, high-collared woollen sweater. Warm looking. Benet had knitted it.

'See if it fits,' he said.

I took off my coat and put on the sweater. It was too big; the sleeves hung down over my hands. But it was warm. I put my coat on over it, and my scarf.

'Thanks,' I said.

'Hmph,' Benet grunted. 'Take a biscuit with you.'

'Thanks,' I said again. I took a biscuit and some cheese and shoved them into my coat pocket. 'I'll be back later,' I said, and left.

I'd be back when I found my locus magicalicus, is what I meant. And if I didn't find it, maybe I wouldn't come back at all.

Secretary Keeston has no initiative, no ideas, no curiosity about magic. Does what he's told and nothing else.

Sent him to fetch books from academicos library. Need to check calibration for partelet because blasted thing not set correctly.

After secretary had gone out, Benet came in with tea, set down plate of biscuits.

Which reminded me. —Tell the boy when he comes in that I want to speak to him, I said. Wanted to tell him to read the treatise on Arhionvar, and then see what he thought about it.

Benet glared. —Don't know that he will come back at all, Magister.

Became aware that secretary had come quietly up stairs and was lurking outside door, listening.

—That is all, Benet, I said. As Benet went out, secretary came in.

Annoyed. Don't like sneaking.

Keeston sat down at the table and took biscuit.

—Magister Nevery, I happened to overhear you and your servant talking about your apprentice. You might be interested to know, sir, that Conn hasn't been attending the academicos for some time. I hear he's been seen going into the Twilight, which must mean, sir, that he's gone back to thieving.

—Get out, I said.

—But sir, squeaked Keeston.

—Out! I stood and pointed at the door.

Keeston scurried out.

Curse it, had forgotten date. Stupid, careless. Checked journal, realized today is thirty days since boy's introduction to magisters. Possible Benet is right, boy will not return to Heartsease.

Curse the boy, anyway. Weather worsening, snow last night, more snow likely. No doubt he is out in the city somewhere, getting himself into trouble.

CHAPTER 20

After I left Heartsease, using the keystone to pass the gates in the tunnels, I came out onto the Night Bridge and turned east. It was about midday, and, as I came out from the bridge and into the city, the Sunrise was bustling.

The streets were clotted with mud and horse manure, all churned with the snow that had fallen the previous night into a dirty, icy slush. My feet were wet within a few steps, and even with Benet's sweater under my coat, the wind was biting. I pulled my scarf up over my face – all the better to hide from the city guards, I reckoned – and headed deeper into the Sunrise.

Most of the buildings in this part of the city were built of grey stone, and the streets were paved with black cobbles. Shops lined the roads, their signs jutting out over the street and creaking in the wind. People, bundled to their ears in warm coats, rushed through the streets, but the richest people travelled in carriages or in hansom cabs pulled by high-stepping horses, whose breath steamed in the chilly air.

I decided to start near the river and work my way up, towards the centre of the city, the hill the Dawn Palace was built on, where the duchess lived.

I paced streets and alleyways for the rest of the day. As I had before, I tried to keep myself open to the merest hint of a call from my locus magicalicus, but I felt nothing. I wasn't sure, anyway, *how* to keep myself open for the call. Was it like listening? Would I just *know*? Would it be, as Brumbee had said, like getting washed away by a wave of magic?

My feet were numb and my socks wet inside my boots, and an icy wind from the river kept knifing me in the back as I trudged along. As the night drew on and wizards came out to light the werelights along the streets, I found a house with a coal hole leading down to a cellar. I pulled my knife out of my boot and used it to pry open the window. Climbed in and found a dark corner to sleep in.

Except that I didn't sleep. I lay there all night, shivering and staring at the darkness, trying to make my thoughts stop whirling around. I still had the biscuit and cheese in my pocket, but I couldn't eat it.

As the light turned grey with morning, I climbed out of the cellar, smudged all over with coal dust. Headed out into the city again.

Trudged. Up one street, down another. The cobbles felt like blocks of ice under my feet. The wind stuck cold fingers down my neck. Overhead, the clouds lowered and snow began to fall, icy pellets like little needles. I felt completely hollow. If somebody had hit me, I would have echoed.

Toward evening, the snowfall grew heavier and I headed up the hill to the centre of the city.

I had my head down, scanning the snow-covered cobbles, with my scarf over my face. A big hand came down on my shoulder.

'Here, you.'

I looked up. A guard. I pulled my scarf down, just a little, to speak. 'I'm running a message.'

'Oh, are you? Let's see it.' The guard held out a gloved hand.

'It's in here,' I said, pointing to my head.

'Where you going to?' the guard said, suspicious.

'The Dawn Palace.' Drats. But it was the only place in the Sunrise that I could think of, hollow as I was.

The guard frowned. 'They're not going to let the likes of you in,' he said.

'Still, that's where I'm going.' Actually, now

that we were talking about the Dawn Palace, I realized that I really did want to go there. Up the hill. Yes. A very good place to go.

The guard shrugged, evidently believing me. 'Get on with you, then.' He took his hand from my shoulder and I skiffed off up the street.

I hadn't eaten anything the previous day, not even the biscuit and cheese, which had disintegrated into crumbs in my pocket, and I hadn't slept during the night and only a few hours the night before, but for some reason I suddenly felt just fine. The worry that had been gnawing at me for the past thirty days took its teeth and went elsewhere. What a relief.

As I went up the hill toward the Dawn Palace, twilight fell and a cloaked wizard with a locus stone went along the street before me making the werelights lining the streets flicker on. The lights gleamed in the growing darkness, making the snowy streets and the grey buildings glow pink. Several carriages passed me as I walked, the horses' breath steaming in the air, their hooves kicking up clots of muddy slush, the wheels rattling over the cobbles.

At last, at the top of the hill, I reached the Dawn Palace, where the duchess lived and governed the city. The carriages had been heading here, too: the duchess was having a party.

At the front of the Dawn Palace was a low wall about half my height topped with a tall, black-iron fence. I gripped the bars, looking in. The palace was a huge rectangular structure built of stone coloured the rosy pink of dawn. All along the front were pillars and frothy carvings; it looked like a cake, frosted and ready to eat. The carriages rolled down the snow-covered drive and pulled up before the front doors, which were reached by going up a broad flight of stairs decorated at the sides with pink stone statues. Werelights flared in sconces at the front, and in their glow I saw fine fur-wrapped ladies and frock-coated gentlemen scurrying from the warm carriages, up the icy steps, and into the warm palace.

My thirty days were up. I would never find my locus magicalicus. I wasn't Nevery's apprentice anymore. I would never be a wizard.

Which meant I was a thief.

Where there were fine ladies and gentlemen, I reckoned, there would be fine jewels and gold and pearls. I would have to find a way in and steal some of them.

Also by the front door were guards, outfitted in thick, dark green woollen uniforms and high leather boots; a few more guards stood at the gates at the head of the driveway, and I was starting to attract their attention, hanging around the fence as I was.

So I eased off down the street to find a nearby alley to wait in until later, when the night would be darker.

I leaned against a wall in an alley for a few hours. Fat snowflakes sifted down from the sky and settled on the ground, and every once in a while a blast of wind came along and stirred the snow into a whirling white frenzy. I jittered while I waited, bouncing up and down, talking to myself.

'I'll go 'round the back,' I told myself. 'And peek in the windows. The guards won't see me. I'll find somebody wearing jewels. And I'll steal them when they aren't looking.'

It seemed like a very good plan.

At last I could wait no longer. It was late, close to midnight, I reckoned, and the party would be in full swing. I crept out of my alley and climbed up the hill to the Dawn Palace.

Away from the front gates, the palace wall got higher and was topped with metal spikes, each spike wearing a little cap of snow. Following the wall around a corner, I found myself in a quiet alley about two paces wide made by the palace wall and a brick building with no windows. A perfect place; no guards in sight. The wall was made of big stone blocks with nice cracks between them. I took off my boots, tied the laces, and hung them around my neck, then climbed up.

At the top of the palace wall, I crouched for a moment, clinging to the spikes, to survey the other side. Blinking snowflakes from my lashes, I saw what looked like a formal garden with snow-covered lumps that were probably hedges and flower beds and winding paths. Across the garden was the side of the palace. All the windows were lit up; it looked like a bright ship sailing on a foamy ocean.

I swung down to hang from my fingertips from the top of the wall, then let go, landing with a crackling of branches and a whump of snow in a bush. Quickly I climbed out, brushing the snow from my coat, and crouched behind the bush, putting my boots back on and tying the laces. Ready, I peered out. Silence, except for the faint sound of music and voices coming from the palace.

I was facing a wide terrace with a low stone wall around it. Along the ground floor were doors made of small windows, which opened right out onto the terrace. The windows were steamed up, so I couldn't see much but bright lights and colours, and movement. It looked warm, inviting.

I crept closer to see.

One of the windowed doors cracked open. A wisp of bright, happy music leaked out and was muffled again as somebody slipped out the door and closed it behind her.

Rowan?

She didn't see me at first. Even though she was only wearing thin slippers, she scuffed through the snow to the terrace wall, where she brushed off the snow and sat down with a tired sigh. She wore a deep green velvet dress with long sleeves and lace at the collar and cuffs. On her hair she wore a wide green velvet band, and she also wore a pearl necklace and eardrops.

I didn't consider even for a moment stealing her jewellery.

I climbed up the wall and dropped onto the terrace in a little cloud of snow.

'Hello, Ro,' I said. 'You look nice.'

She looked startled for a moment, and then she gave me her down-the-nose smile. 'Connwaer. How lovely to see you.'

It was good to see her, actually. I grinned back.

'I suppose I ought to ask you what you're doing here,' she said, her breath steaming in the freezing air.

I shrugged and sat beside her. 'I could ask you the same thing.'

'Mmm, I expect you would, Conn.'

'It's a very fancy party,' I said.

Rowan gazed at the bright windows. 'Very fancy.'

'Lots of fine ladies and gentlemen,' I said.

She shot me a sharp sideways glance. 'What are you up to?'

'Nothing,' I said. 'Just curious.'

'Oh, I imagine so. Would you like to see better?'

I definitely would. I nodded.

Rowan got to her feet. Snowflakes had settled on her flame-coloured hair and on her dress. 'Over here.'

She led me across the terrace to a long window at the end, which wasn't as steamed up as the others. I peeked in. Chandeliers, whirling couples, green trees in pots, garlands of flowers.

And then, across the ballroom, on a necklace worn by a woman sitting on a carved, fancy chair, I saw it. A jewel, green and sparkling. The most perfect jewel in the entire world.

Secretary and I in workroom, adjusting cursed partelet on gauge. Distracted. Boy's dratted cat yowling about the place.

Too much to do, not enough time. Must determine whether loss of magic is natural or not.

Sent Benet to find boy so cat will be quiet and I can get some work done.

CHAPTER 21

Even from outside and across the room, I could see it absolutely clearly. The jewel was about as big as the palm of my hand, leaf shaped and leaf coloured, and faceted all over so that it glittered in the light.

'Are you ever coming back to the academicos?' Rowan asked.

The jewel was the centrepiece of the lady's necklace, which looked like it was made of diamonds and smaller green jewels, but I didn't care about the other stuff, only the one that was mine, the leaf jewel.

'Conn?' Rowan asked.

What? Oh, the academicos. 'I don't know,' I said. 'D'you see that lady over there?' I pointed. The woman was sitting on a fancy chair, speaking to some people gathered around her. She wore a dark green dress similar to Rowan's, and my jewel glimmered against the green, almost as if it was calling to me.

Rowan leaned over to follow where my finger was pointing. 'Yes, I see her.'

'D'you know where she lives?' I could sneak into her house, wherever it was, and steal the jewel after she'd gone to sleep. Easy.

'She lives here,' Rowan said. She looked at me with a half smile on her face. 'She's the duchess.'

Oh. Right. Well then, I wouldn't have far to go, would I? All I had to do was wait for the party to end, and in I would go. It'd be risky, but it'd be worth it to get the jewel.

At the other end of the terrace, one of the

windowed doors opened. 'Lady Rowan?' a deep voice called, accompanied by light music and laughter from the party.

Before he saw me, I ducked behind Rowan, then went over the low wall, where I crouched in the shadows.

Up on the terrace, Rowan scuffed around. Erasing my footprints, I guessed. 'Yes, I'm here, Argent,' she said. She sounded annoyed. 'I needed a breath of air.'

'You should come in. The night is exceedingly cold.'

It wasn't *that* cold.

Rowan murmured something in response, and they went in, the door closing with a polite *click* behind them.

The night felt suddenly very empty. Snow wafted down from overhead, and the party windows shed their bright lights across the shadowed garden.

I needed someplace quiet and dark to wait until everybody went home and the Dawn Palace went to sleep.

The wall where I'd come in was as good a

place as any. Staying close to the shadows, I crept through the garden and back to the wall, where I settled behind a bush.

The night deepened. The snow stopped falling and the clouds drew off, leaving the sky velvet-black and pricked with stars. The cold seeped into my bones, but I couldn't manage to care about it. The lights from the party went out, one by one, and the faint sound of music and laughter faded away. I got to my feet and paced back and forth behind my bush, my hand on the wall to steady myself. Every part of me tingled with excitement, like tiny needles pricking over my skin, making my hair stand up on end and my fingers twitch.

It was time.

I took off my coat and scarf because the black sweater Benet had knitted for me would blend more easily with the shadows. Quick-quiet, I eased from behind the bush and ran lightly across the garden, and then up onto the terrace to the windowed doors. I crouched there for a moment. Nothing moved in the garden. Stars glittered overhead. Beyond the palace, the faintest touch of grey stained the eastern sky; morning wasn't too far off. No matter. I'd be in and out in minutes. I knew exactly where the leaf jewel was.

I tried the door, but it was locked, so I pulled out my knife and stuck it in the lock. It turned, smooth as butter, and the door clicked open. I slid inside, closing the door behind me.

I was in a ballroom, huge and dark and echoey, smelling faintly of sweat and leftover flowers from the party. I took off my boots and socks and put them next to the door where I could pick them up on my way out. Keeping to the edge of the ballroom, I barefooted to a dark doorway, which led in the direction of my jewel, and paused to listen.

Nothing, only silence.

I eased into the shadowed hallway and wound my way deeper into the palace. I turned a corner, then another, and went up a flight of stairs. I met no one, saw no lights. I came to yet another corner and peeked around, finding a long, carpeted hallway lit by a single werelight turned low; halfway along the hall was a door, which was blocked by a huge, alert guardsman wearing a green uniform and holding a pike. As I snuck another look at him, he turned his head to survey the hallway, and I drew back into the shadows, holding my breath.

Drats. That guard was a lock I could not pick.

But the leaf jewel was behind that door. Which meant I had to get in. Find a window, maybe, and go in from outside? Try to distract the guard? Hide and wait for daytime and hope the door would be left unguarded?

No, I couldn't wait. The jewel wanted me to come and get it *now*.

Then my problem was solved for me.

In the distance, from outside the palace, came a faint shout. It was answered a moment later from inside.

Peering around the corner, I saw the guard stiffen and grip his pike. The noises from below grew louder: shouting, then someone ringing a bell. From the other end of the hallway, another guardsman poked his head in and called the guard in front of the door. 'All clear, Jas?'

The jewel's guard stepped away from the

door and faced the other guard. 'Clear. That you, Merik? What's going on?'

In my hiding place around the corner, I crouched, ready to go. Just one more step, guard, and I'd have enough space to reach the door. Just one more step . . .

The other guard answered. 'Gate guards found footprints in the snow by the garden wall. Captain Kerrn has called an alert. We're searching the grounds and the palace now.'

Drats. I'd forgotten about footprints. Stupid.

The door guard took a few more steps toward the other guard. 'Well, everything's quiet up here—'

That's all I needed.

Quick as thought, I darted from around my corner, down the hallway, to the door. I had the knife in my hand and jammed it into the lock as the guard turned; the lock flicked open, and as he lunged to grab me, I was in, with the door slammed behind me and the knife snicking the lock closed again.

I whirled, panting, and surveyed the room. Dark, curtained windows, stone floor, gilded pictures, padded chairs, and a desk.

And standing beside a canopied bed was the duchess, her eyes wide, her grey-streaked red hair in two braids, a lit candle in one hand and a knife in the other.

'Who are you and what do you want?' she asked sharply. The candle flame flickered, sending shadows reeling across the walls and ceiling.

She said something else, but I could hardly hear her. The jewel's call was so loud.

From behind me, the door thudded with the guards' blows. One of them shouted for help.

My eyes were drawn toward a carved wooden box on a table across the room.

Yes, of course it was there. Its call washed over me like a crashing wave.

I crossed the room to the box. It was locked. I didn't have time for this. 'Keys?' I asked.

The duchess, who had not moved from beside the bed, looked down her nose, proud. 'I will not give you the keys.'

Oh well, the knife had worked fine so far. I stuck it into the keyhole and it didn't so much turn the lock as explode it, as if the jewel inside wanted to get out as much as I wanted to get in. The lid of the box burst open. Behind me, the duchess's door shuddered with the guards' efforts to get in.

Inside the box, the necklace was arrayed against a lining of dark green velvet. And in the centre of the necklace, the leaf-green jewel glimmered as if it was lit from within. I reached in and cut it from the necklace with my knife, prying it from its setting. It came into my hand as if it was part of me. I was meant to have it.

From behind, the door splintered open. The guards bulled into the room, shouting.

'He's got a knife!' somebody yelled.

As I turned, a heavy weight hit me and I crashed to the floor with a guardsman on top of me. The knife – *and my jewel* – flew out of my hands and skittered across the polished stone floor. The guard held me down, and I struggled, kicking and twisting; I bit a guard's hand and his grip relaxed for a moment and I squirmed away.

Then there was a flash of light, a pain in my head, and I was out.

CHAPTER 22

When I came to, the call of the jewel had faded so that I could barely feel it. But it was nearby, so I figured I was still in the Dawn Palace somewhere. Just not in the nice part.

I was sitting in a hard chair with my hands chained behind me. My head hurt. I opened my eyes. Damp, grey stone walls. No windows. A werelight in a metal lantern cast flickering shadows across the room. Two fierce-looking guards.

I was in big trouble.

One of the guards, a big man with a bristling grey and black beard, noticed that I was awake. 'He's up,' he said. 'I'll give him the phlister. Call Captain Kerrn.'

'Right,' said the other, and left the room.

The remaining guard went to a table, where he poured out a mug of water, to which he added a powder from a vial. He stirred it with a finger, then carried it over to me.

'Drink this,' he said.

I eyed the water. It looked greasy, with a film of powder on the surface. I was thirsty, but I wasn't drinking this stuff. I shook my head.

The guard grabbed me by the scruff of my neck. 'You drink it,' he growled, 'or I force it down your throat.'

Which is what he managed to do, eventually. I came out of it gasping and choking and wet down the front of my sweater, and he got his shins kicked.

I expected the phlister to be bitter, like poison maybe, but it didn't taste like anything except water.

After a short time, which I spent contemplating the lock on the door and testing the manacles on my wrists, the captain arrived.

She was tall – all the guards were tall; they must have a height requirement – and had blonde hair in a braid down her back and hard grey-blue eyes like chips of ice. She wore the same dark green uniform as the other guards, with a gold stripe stitched on one sleeve. 'Has he had the phlister?' the captain asked.

'I could pick that lock with a couple of wires,' I said, pointing with my chin toward the door. 'And I've got two wires in the collar of my shirt.'

Now why had I told them that?

The guard and the captain looked at me. 'I see he has,' Captain Kerrn said. 'Wait outside.' Her words sounded funny, the *r*'s all gargled in the back of her throat and the *s*'s pronounced 'sh.'

The guard nodded and went out, the door locking behind him.

The captain stood with her arms folded, glaring down at me.

'You can glare all you want,' I said. 'But I'm used to it. Benet does it all the time.'

'What is your name?' the captain asked.

'Conn,' I said promptly. 'Connwaer, actually. It's a kind of bird with black feathers. I don't usually tell people that.' I gave her a suspicious look. 'Did the phlister make me tell you?'

'I ask the questions,' Kerrn said. 'You answer them. Why did you try to assassinate the duchess? Who are you working for?'

I blinked and stared at her. 'Why would I want to kill the duchess?'

'You tell me, Connwaer.' The captain leaned forward and spoke in a soft, menacing voice. 'Why would you want to kill the duchess?'

I considered the question. 'Well, maybe if I was crazy I would. Or maybe if I thought she was truly evil?' I shook my head. 'Even then, I don't think I'd actually try to kill her.'

Captain Kerrn narrowed her eyes. 'So you were not trying to kill the duchess.'

'No!' I said. 'Why did you think I was?'

The captain relaxed ever so slightly and leaned against the table. 'You were captured in her chamber, with a knife.'

I nodded. 'That's right. I had to get the jewel.'

At that, Captain Kerrn straightened. 'You mean the ducal regalia.'

'No,' I said. I shifted in the chair, which had gotten harder. 'I mean the jewel. The one that glimmers green, like a leaf in the sunlight? It's beautiful. D'you know the one I mean?'

'Yes, I know it,' Kerrn said. 'Go on.'

'It's mine,' I said.

'No,' the captain said. 'It is part of the ducal regalia.'

'No,' I said firmly. 'It's mine.'

'Who asked you to steal it? Are you working for the Underlord?'

'Nobody asked me to, Kerrn. It's mine.' I shook my head, frustrated. 'Clear as clear, I have to tell you the truth because of this phlister stuff. So why don't you believe me?'

The captain scowled. 'Because you are asking too many questions.' She turned and paced across the cell and back. 'The phlister is not working,' she said to herself.

'It's working,' I said. 'You're just not asking

the right questions.'

Kerrn took two quick steps across the room and grabbed me by the front of my sweater. 'Then tell me the right questions.'

I thought about that for a moment, while Kerrn released me and folded her arms, waiting. The right questions.

'I haven't even asked myself the right questions,' I said slowly. 'Conn,' I asked. 'Why did you break into the Dawn Palace?'

'To find the jewel,' I told myself.

'But *why*?' I asked.

And the answer washed over me like a flood of sunlight filling every crack and corner of the damp, dim room. Of course. How could I have been so stupid? I looked up at the captain, the happiness bubbling up inside of me.

'I had to find the leaf jewel, Kerrn. It really is mine. I'm a wizard, and it's my locus magicalicus.'

Brumbee came, worried about boy, who hasn't been going to school. Stayed for dinner.

Benet came in. Said guard had come to Night Bridge with message: boy's been arrested at the Dawn Palace, Magister Nevery is called for.

First thought was relief. Boy not dead, at least. Brumbee asked what the boy had done.

—Arrested for stealing a jewel from the duchess's regalia, Benet said.

Brumbee. —Oh, I'm so sorry, Nevery.

Stared at him. —For what?

Brumbee dithered. Then, —Conn's returned to thievery, hasn't he?

Thievery? Highly unlikely. Far better explanation for his actions than thievery.

—Brumbee, I said. —My apprentice has finally found his locus magicalicus. Are you coming?

Yes, he was.

CHAPTER 23

*C*aptain Kerrn decided that the first dose of phlister hadn't worked. I told her it had, but she didn't believe me. So they gave me another.

This time they tied my feet together, so I got a bloody lip and wet down the front of my sweater again, but nobody got kicked.

Then Kerrn and the bristle-bearded guard, whose name was Farn, took turns asking me questions. The same questions, over and over, for hours.

I told them the truth, and they continued to not believe me.

I didn't mind about any of it. I'd found my locus magicalicus. 'I really am a wizard,' I told them, and soon Nevery would come and explain everything, I'd get my locus stone, and I'd go home to Heartsease. I'd go to the academicos, Brumbee would be plumply pleased, Lady would purr, Benet would bake biscuits, and Rowan and I would be friends again.

'I don't want to hear any more about the damn biscuits,' Farn said to the captain. 'We're not going to get anything else out of him, Captain. We'd better bring in this Magister Nevery.'

Kerrn nodded. 'Get the lockpicks out of his collar, Farn, and stay with him just in case.' She stalked out of the cell, slamming the door behind her.

At first the guard was close-mouthed, but after I told him how to find the wires sewn inside my shirt collar, he got more talkative. When I asked how long I'd been there, he told me a day and a half. He said that yes, there was a height requirement for palace guards. He also said that the punishment for attempting to kill the duchess was death by hanging, but I explained that I hadn't, in fact, tried to kill the duchess, so I wasn't worried. He said I should be.

After a while, I was starting to feel stretched very thin. I hadn't eaten in days, or slept.

I found myself talking about Benet's biscuits again.

'All right!' Farn said. 'I'll get you something to eat.' He stood up and went to the door. 'Anything to get you to stop talking.'

And out he went. As soon as the door closed behind him, I brought my chained hands from behind my back, under my legs, and up to the front where I could get a better look at the manacles. The lock was a simple twisted plunger; I had just the thing for it. I felt down the seams of my trousers to where I'd hidden another set of lockpick wires. After bending them into the right shapes, I picked the manacle lock and had my hands free. Then I untied my feet.

Getting up from my chair, I went to the door and listened. No one on the outside, it sounded like. The door gave me no more trouble than the manacles had, just a quick-snick, and the lock clicked over. Time to go get my locus magicalicus. Its call had grown more insistent; it knew I was nearby, and it wanted me to come and fetch it.

I cracked open the door and peered out.

The guard Farn stood in the room outside with a tray of food and a jug of water, looking over his shoulder at Captain Kerrn, who was entering the room through an arched door. And behind her came Benet and—

'Hello, Nevery!' I said, pushing the door wide and stepping out of my cell.

Nevery gave me an exasperated look – I knew it well – but before he could say anything, Farn dropped the tray with a crash and Captain Kerrn strode across the room, grabbed me by the collar, dragged me back into the cell, and chained my hands in front of me. Then she threw me into the chair and stood glaring down at me.

Nevery came to the doorway. Benet loomed up behind him, also glaring. Not at me, for a change, but at Kerrn.

'I knew you'd come, Nevery,' I said. I started to get up from the chair, but Kerrn shoved me back again.

'Sit *down*,' she growled.

I grinned at Nevery. 'They said you wouldn't come, but I told them you would. "My master will come and get me," I said.'

'Oh, so I'm your master now, am I, boy?' He spoke to Kerrn. 'He is my apprentice, Captain. Release him.'

'Nevery, they arrested me because I tried to steal a jewel from the duchess's necklace—'

'Be quiet, boy.' Nevery pointed at the chains on my hands. 'Go on,' he ordered the captain. 'Take them off.'

Kerrn shook her head. 'Not without an order from the duchess.'

'—Nevery,' I interrupted. 'I don't think you should let me out of here, because if you do, I'll try to steal it again. I know I shouldn't, but that's what I'll do, sure as sure.'

'What's the matter with you, boy?' Nevery asked. He studied me, frowning. 'You're chattering.'

'Phlister,' said Captain Kerrn.

'It makes people tell the truth all the time,' I said.

'Hmph,' Nevery said. 'You were given phlister? That would seem to be redundant.'

'What d'you mean?' I asked.

'I mean that you tell the truth already.'

'No I don't, Nevery. I lie to you all the time.'

'Be quiet, boy.' He turned and spoke to Benet, behind him. 'Go see what's taking Brumbee so long.'

'Yes, Master,' Benet said. He paused and looked me over. 'You all right?'

'Yes,' I said. 'I'm very glad to see you, Benet.'

'Don't listen to him,' said Nevery. 'Just go.'

'Nevery,' I said. 'I *have* lied to you.'

'Oh, really,' Nevery said. 'Name once, boy. Maybe thinking about that will keep you quiet for a while.' He pointed at the door and said to Benet, 'Go!'

Benet left. After a quick glance at me, Nevery

leaned on his cane and stared at the floor, and Captain Kerrn moved to stand blocking the door. I tried to count the number of times that I had lied to Nevery.

And I couldn't think of a single instance. In the Twilight I had been a thief, which basically meant *liar*. But ever since meeting Nevery, though there were some things I hadn't told him about, I had never lied to him because I hadn't *needed* to lie about anything.

As I was about to explain this to Nevery, Benet returned, Brumbee trailing behind him, looking worried.

'Hello, Brumbee!' I said.

'Yes, hello, Conn,' Brumbee said. 'I'm glad to see you're all right. We've been very worried about you.' He turned his attention to Nevery. 'The duchess requires that we all appear before her. I tried to explain about the' – he lowered his voice so only Nevery and I could hear – 'about what Conn claims is his locus magicalicus, but I'm not sure she believed me.' He shot me a worried look. 'Nevery, I'm not sure *I* believe it. No wizard has ever possessed a locus stone of that size and quality.'

Nevery shrugged. 'If the duchess wants it proven, then it shall be proven.'

Oh, so Nevery had figured out about my locus magicalicus. I didn't have to explain. I opened my mouth to say more about my locus stone, but Nevery interrupted.

'Be quiet, boy, if you can.' He gestured to Brumbee. 'We'll speak to the duchess, and you' – he pointed at Captain Kerrn, who scowled back at him – 'will bring the boy up in a few minutes. Wait outside the door until you are called. Let us go.'

And he swept-stepped from the room, his cane going *tap tap* on the stone floor. Brumbee and Benet followed him.

After they'd gone, Captain Kerrn practised her glare on me, and Farn joined her at it, standing in the doorway with his arms folded.

I ignored them. Which wasn't hard, because my locus magicalicus was telling me very strongly that it didn't want to wait much longer for me to find it. Before, I'd wondered what the call of my locus stone would sound like. It wasn't like a call at all. More like a kind of intense pull, a deep drumming hum in the heavier bones of my legs and in my skull, and a light and tingling buzz in the small bones of my fingers and toes.

Sitting still in the chair was very difficult.

Fortunately, I didn't have to sit for very long.

'It has been long enough,' Captain Kerrn said. 'Bring him, Farn.'

I jumped up and Farn grabbed me by the back of my sweater and shoved me out, following Kerrn. I would have gone myself, because the pull from my locus stone was getting stronger, and we were going in the right direction. They brought me to a double door with a green-coated guard standing in front of it. The call from my locus stone was making my whole body vibrate. 'Can you hear that?' I asked Farn, who still had a grip on my sweater. He scowled and didn't answer.

One of the double doors swung open and Brumbee stuck his head out. 'You may bring him in now,' he said, and opened the door wider.

Farn and I followed Captain Kerrn into the room, an office, it looked like, crowded with chairs and tables with lace doilies on them and trees in pots; the captain nodded to the duchess, who sat in a chair carved of dark wood behind a wide, polished desk piled with books and papers. Rowan stood beside the duchess's desk. Nevery was there, too, leaning on his cane and looking annoyed, and Benet and Brumbee, along with a few more tall palace guards. Farn shoved me before the duchess and kicked the back of my leg to make me kneel. From the stone floor, I looked up at her. She leaned across the desk and stared down her nose at me, pale and icy cold and very beautiful.

The duchess straightened and said something. Nevery's gravelly voice said something back. I shook my head, trying to hear, but the stone's call grew louder. I started to get up, but Farn put his hand on my shoulder and held me down. The stone was in the corner, behind one of the duchess's guards. Somewhere over there. I squirmed, but Farn tightened his grip on me.

Then somebody said something, and he let me go.

Call call call, went my locus stone. I wobbled

to my feet. 'All right, I'm coming,' I said. I crossed the room, past the staring duchess and Rowan, past Nevery and Brumbee, and ducked around a guard. There, in the corner, behind a table.

I went down on my knees and lifted up the edge of a fringed rug, and there it was. Even in the dark corner, my locus magicalicus glowed against the stone floor, just as I'd remembered it – leaf shaped, leaf green, faceted, and glimmering. When I picked it up, it felt glad, coming home, heavy and solid in my hand.

I got to my feet and turned around, and they were all staring at me. Nevery was trying to hide a smile in his beard.

'I suppose that proves it,' Brumbee said.

Captain Kerrn looked ready to boil over. 'It was a trick. Magister Nevery signalled to the thief, told him where the stone was hidden.'

They all turned to the duchess to see what she would say. But she stared across the room at me. Her face was proud and pale, and as she looked me up and down, the curl of her lip told me she didn't like what she saw. I knew what I must look like to her: tangled hair, bare feet, smudged with coal dust, the jewel from her necklace in my chained hands. A thief.

But then she slowly shook her head. 'Magister Nevery did not know where the jewel was hidden. This boy found it himself.'

'And his affinity for the stone is easily proven,' said Nevery. He nodded at me. 'Do some magic.'

Magic, right. I'd seen Nevery do the light spell plenty of times, so I held up the stone and called out the spell: *'Lothfalas!'*

The magic burst forth in a flood, cresting through me and then crashing out, filling the room. My locus stone blazed like lightning frozen in the moment of striking; the bones of my hands glowed red, clenched around the stone. The manacles burst open and exploded into a swarm of sparks. The rest of my body lit up with white-bright flames that flickered and danced, but didn't burn. The others in the room flinched away, covering their faces.

Nevery took a step toward me, raising his hand to shield his eyes.

I caught my breath. 'How do I stop it?' I asked. My voice sounded squeaky and a little bit frightened.

'Just will it to stop, boy,' he said calmly.

Right. I closed my eyes against the flames and light and willed the magic back. And it went.

When I opened my eyes, the brightness had receded; the locus magicalicus was just a leaf-shaped, spring-green jewel in my hand.

The others were blinking the brights from their eyes to stare at me. The duchess looked shaken and Rowan's eyes were shining.

'Well,' said Brumbee. 'That answers that question, doesn't it, Nevery?'

Nevery was looking at me with an odd smile on his face. 'It does, indeed,' he answered. To me, he said, 'That was quite a display, boy.'

I gave Nevery a shaky grin. I was a wizard, clear as clear.

Boy has claimed his locus magicalicus. Quite a remarkable display.

Afterward, Benet and I brought him home. Sat him down on a stool in the kitchen, still chattering, clutching his locus stone, talking to the cat, to Benet, and mostly to me.

Benet brought tea. Asked, —He going to stop soon?

I watched boy. —Wait for it, I said.

The boy ate three biscuits with butter, then jumped up to pace around the room, telling Benet and me that he hadn't realized that Rowan was the duchess's daughter, when he stopped dead, as if he'd run into a stone wall. A look of utter surprise and confusion crossed his face.

Benet glanced at me. I nodded. —Catch him.

The boy's eyes dropped closed and he swayed where he stood. Benet stepped up and caught him as he toppled over.

—Put him to bed, I said.

CHAPTER 24

In the morning, I woke up as usual in my attic room, snuggled in blankets. The room was freezing. The air went into my lungs like shards of ice and came out again as puffs of white steam. My nose was cold. A layer of ice crystals covered the blankets. If I'd spent a night this cold on the streets of the Twilight, I would have woken up huddled and frozen

241

in a doorway. Or not woken up at all. It was good to be home.

Outside, the wind shrieked around the corner of the house, and the sky, what I could see of it through my windows, was grey.

And my locus magicalicus was lost in the blankets somewhere. I rooted around until I found it. Then, hugging the blankets around me, I sat up, leaned against the wall, and held the stone up to the light. It glowed from within, a shifting, dappled warmth like sunlight shining down through the leaves of tall trees.

No other wizard had ever had a locus magicalicus like this. Most jewel locus stones were smaller, Nevery had told me. Large jewels were dangerous; hadn't he said that, too? Sure as sure, my locus stone was the most valuable jewel in the city, maybe in all the Peninsular Duchies. Why had it come to me? It didn't make sense.

Maybe Nevery would know.

Oh, well. Time to get up. Untangling myself from the blankets, I felt a little stiff and sore from the past few days, and the back of my head hurt a little from where the duchess's guards had bashed me. But nothing too bad, considering.

To my surprise, my coat and black sweater were folded neatly on the floor, my boots and socks lined up beside them. The last time I'd seen them, I'd been sneaking into the Dawn Palace. Shivering, I put them on, put my locus magicalicus into my coat pocket, and went downstairs to the kitchen.

Benet wasn't up yet. I raked up the banked fires in the stove and the fireplace, added wood, then grabbed the bucket and went out to fetch water. I paused on the threshold to wrap my scarf around my face and to pull the sleeves of my coat over my hands.

As I stepped out the door, the wind raced 'round the corner of the house and struck with icy daggers down into my bones, almost knocking me off my feet. Tiny flecks of snow, whipped by the wind, scudded across the courtyard. In the tree, the birds balanced on the branches with their backs to the wind, looking ruffled and annoyed.

Catching my breath, I set off toward the well. The birds caught sight of me. With a sudden cackling and cawing, they leaped from the branches, spattering the ground with their droppings, shedding feathers, which spun away in the wind. In a clackety-rackety black cloud, they raced across the courtyard to where I stood holding the bucket and swirled around me, chattering loudly, brushing me with the soft tips of their wings. I dropped the bucket. They whirled up like a fluttering funnel of black rags, and then flew back to the tree, where they settled onto the branches.

I stood staring at them and they stared back, cackling quietly, fluffing their feathers.

I'd never heard of birds acting like that. Strange. With an eye on their tree, I picked up the bucket, went to the well and fetched water, then went back to the house and climbed the stairs to the kitchen. Benet was there, sitting at the table with his hair standing up in spikes all over his head.

'G'morning,' I said, and carried the bucket to the stove, where I filled the kettle.

Benet glared at me, which made me happy. I took off my coat and started to get the tea ready.

'Can I see it?' Benet asked.

My locus magicalicus, he meant. I went over to my coat, fetched out the jewel, and put it on the table, then went back to the stove to pour hot water into the teapot.

When I brought Benet his cup of tea, he was studying the stone, but not touching it. 'It dangerous?' he asked.

I fetched a chair and sat down next to him. I picked up the stone. It felt cool and just a little prickly; if it were a cat, it would have its back arched and its fur on end, but it wouldn't hiss or scratch. 'I don't think so,' I said. When I'd tried to steal Nevery's locus magicalicus, it had attacked me, and I figured that if anybody tried to steal mine it would probably kill them. But it wouldn't hurt Benet.

'Hmph,' Benet grunted. He rubbed his hands through his hair and then took a drink of tea. 'Wood,' he said.

Right. I got up, put my locus stone in my pocket, and fetched more wood for the stove and the fireplace. When I'd finished that, Benet had woken up enough to make biscuits, and when those were done I ate three of them with jam and cheese.

Then I took tea and biscuits up to Nevery.

I peeked into the study and he was there, a fat book open on the table before him.

'Breakfast, Nevery,' I said, setting the tray on the table.

He glanced up. Frowned. 'Have you washed?'

I grinned at him. 'No.'

He pointed at the door.

After washing and dressing in my attic room, I picked up the empty water bucket and went downstairs to the kitchen.

Keeston was there. He was sitting at the table watching Benet fry bacon and potatoes on the stove. He'd put his feet up on one of the other chairs and had a book propped on his knees, and he had butter on his fingers from the biscuit he was eating.

I went in and put the empty bucket by the door.

'Shouldn't you fetch more water?' Keeston asked.

I looked at Benet.

'Kettle's full,' Benet said.

I sat down on the floor beside the fireplace, and Lady climbed into my lap, purring.

'So you decided to come back,' Keeston said. He closed his book and set it on the table amid a scattering of biscuit crumbs.

'I always wanted to,' I said.

'I hear you've been going to the Twilight,' Keeston said.

Now where had he heard that? From Pettivox? Drats. Sure as sure, Keeston was spying for his master. Which meant everything he heard was going straight to the Underlord.

So I didn't say anything to Keeston, just shrugged.

Benet clattered a pan on the stove. When I looked up, he glared at me, then jerked his chin at Keeston.

He wanted me to tell about my locus magicalicus. I wanted to show it off to Keeston, make his eyes bulge out with surprise and envy. But it might be better, I reckoned, if he didn't know about it. Because then Crowe wouldn't know about it.

'I went to the Twilight,' I said, 'because I was

looking for my locus stone.'

'And did you find it?' Keeston asked. 'Bring me a plate of that bacon you're cooking,' he said to Benet.

I nodded.

Keeston blinked, then recovered his sneer. 'A common pebble, I suppose.' He fingered his own locus magicalicus, the shard of shiny black rock he'd hung from a gold chain around his neck, just as his master did. 'Something you found on the roadside.'

I shrugged, not yes, not no.

Benet slammed the pan on the stovetop, then dished out three plates of potatoes and bacon, handed one to me where I sat by the fire, thumped one down before Keeston, and sat down with the third at the table.

Keeston picked up a fork from the plate and took a bite. Then he spit it out with a curse. 'Ow! It's hot!' He shot Benet an accusing look.

Benet ignored him.

Setting down his fork, Keeston looked over at where I sat before the fire. 'Well, I suppose it's a good thing you found your little locus pebble.

It may not be very powerful, but at least you'll be of some use to your master.'

I nodded and fished a bit of bacon from my plate. After blowing on it to cool it, I offered it to Lady. She sniffed at it, then uncurled herself from my lap and padded away, so I ate it.

When I looked up, I realized that Nevery was standing in the doorway. 'Well, boy,' he said mildly. 'Eating all the bacon, are you?'

'Most of it,' Benet growled.

At the table, Keeston sat up straight and alert. 'Are you ready to begin working, Magister Nevery?'

Nevery looked thoughtfully at him. Under his gaze, Keeston drooped. 'I have business at Magisters Hall,' Nevery said after a moment. 'You will stay here and continue collating and numbering my notes.' He switched his attention to me. I was eating fast, because I knew Nevery was not going to wait around, and I liked bacon almost as much as I liked biscuits. 'And you, boy,' he said. 'When you've finished eating all the bacon on the island, fetch your books. We're going to the academicos.'

CHAPTER 25

Nevery and I left the house. 'You didn't tell Keeston about your locus magicalicus,' he said. He held onto his hat with one hand and steadied himself with his cane as we slipped and slid across the snowy

courtyard, buffeted by an icy wind.

I shook my head and pulled my scarf down to answer him. 'I didn't think it was a good idea.'

'Because you still suspect Pettivox.'

I nodded.

'Well, boy, you do cling tightly to an idea once it enters your head.'

So did he.

We went down the tunnel stairs, out of the wind. Nevery paced on, me beside him, until we reached the Heartsease gate. In the faint light from the mouth of the tunnel behind us, I could see the carving in the stone beneath our feet: the winged hourglass.

Nevery shot me one of his keen-gleam looks. 'You've seen me open the gates before, boy. Do you remember the opening spells?'

I nodded.

'Then open it.' Nevery pointed with his cane at the gate.

I dug the locus magicalicus out of my pocket. In the dimness of the tunnel, it glowed, shreds of greenish light leaking out from between my fingers. I raised it and called out the opening word: *'Sessamay!'*

A beam of white-bright light exploded from my locus stone and, trailing green sparks, crashed into the lock. The gate burst open, leaping back on its hinges, rebounding with a clang from the tunnel wall, and slamming shut. Bluish sparks ran twinkling up and down the bars and the lock spat out a few glowing embers.

The tunnel fell silent as the echoes faded away. Nevery shook his head. 'Hmph,' he said. 'Try again.'

I took a deep breath, told the magic to behave itself, and spoke the opening spell. As before, the bright lights, the crashing, the sparks, but this time, Nevery stuck his knob-headed cane through the opening before the gate could slam shut again.

We blasted through all the gates along the tunnel to the academicos. At the stairs, Nevery leaned on his cane and looked down at me. 'Now, boy. Go to school. I have a meeting to attend at Magisters Hall.'

Right. He swept away, the *tap tap* of his cane on the stone floor echoing down the tunnel. I went up the stairs to the academicos.

Rowan was waiting for me at the top, wrapped in a warm black coat with her grey student's robe peeking out from underneath it. Her head was swathed in a grey-and-green-striped woollen scarf, and the tip of her nose was red.

'G'morning, Ro,' I said.

She nodded and fell into step beside me. The freezing wind blew fiercely across the academicos courtyard; beyond the island, chunks of ice bobbed by on the surface of the rushing black water of the river. We put our heads down and pushed on; my hands and face felt frozen solid by the time we reached the entryway of the academicos and went in.

The gallery was crowded with grey-robed students, gathered here instead of out in the freezing courtyard, waiting for the first class of the morning to begin. A few of them glanced our way, then returned to their chattering conversations.

Rowan was unwrapping her scarf. 'Do you have it with you?' she asked quietly.

My locus magicalicus, she meant. I nodded.

'What are you going to do about it?'

Leave it to Rowan to get right to the point. 'Not tell anyone,' I said.

She nodded and unbuttoned her coat.

'Is she very angry?' I asked. 'Your mother?'

Rowan looked away. 'I don't know. Sometimes it's hard to tell.'

Around us, the groups of students started to break up and leave the gallery; the first class was about to begin. A student bumped into Rowan and apologized. We couldn't talk here.

Rowan shrugged and we walked together to the apprentices' classroom, where Periwinkle taught us a spell for lighting candles. I figured I'd be able to use it if I ever needed to turn a candle into a smoldering puddle of wax.

When we came out of the classroom, a worried Brumbee was waiting. The duchess, he said, had sent for me.

'I've contacted Nevery, but he is busy at Magisters Hall and asked me to pass on to you a few words of advice. The first one I'm not sure I understand. He says to tell you that the duchess is like a puzzle lock.'

Tricky, Nevery meant. *Be careful, and don't trust her.* I slipped my hand into my coat pocket, just to check on my locus magicalicus, though I knew it was there.

'His second, ah, request is that you don't do any magic. And next, don't tell her anything.'

'I don't know anything, Brumbee.'

'Ah, well, perhaps Nevery thinks you do.' He wrung his hands. 'And last, he said to come home to Heartsease when she's finished with you.'

It sounded like he thought the duchess was going to eat me for dinner.

Arrived at Magisters Hall, went in to meeting. Pettivox not present. Just as well, as man annoys me to no end. Magisters asked about my research on magical decay.

Told them about possible precedent, the lost mountain city of Arhionvar. —We have found textual evidence, I said. —The loss of magic in Arhionvar was precipitous; the city was abandoned in a matter of weeks.

Told them that when I have completed my gauge, I should be able to report further on the situation and what, exactly, we might do about it.

Much work to do before then.

Note to self: Must remember to speak to boy about dangers of jewel locus stones.

CHAPTER 26

On the way up the hill to the Dawn Palace, I thought about why the duchess might want to see me.

Did she think I could help deal with the decay of magic? I wanted to help, but as Nevery would be the first to point out, I had no abilities beyond opening gates, making light, and turning myself into a cat, which I wasn't even sure I could do yet, though I wanted to try it.

The next thought turned my stomach cold, as I walked through the front gate before the Dawn Palace, my feet crunching through crusted snow. The duchess disliked Nevery enough to banish him from the city for twenty years. Was she after Nevery, then? Did she think I would tell her something about Nevery's work?

I shook my head and paid attention to where I was going. When I'd been here before, it had been night and snow had been sifting down from a sky made pink and soft by flickering werelights. Now the snow-covered drive leading up to the front steps of the Dawn Palace had been trodden into a slippery, icy path. I slithered up the front steps, which had been shovelled and sanded, to the double front doors, where two green-coated, leather-booted guards stood with pikes.

'That him?' one of the guards said.

The door handle turned easily, but before I could push the door open and go in, a heavy hand came down on my shoulder.

'Here, you,' said a guard.

I looked up. Tall and bearded, but not one of the guards from the cells below the Dawn

Palace. 'I'm supposed to see the duchess,' I said.

'I'll take him,' the guard with the grip on me said to the other. He opened the door and pushed me inside. 'Come quietly.' He pulled me along by my arm through the main hall, turning left into a carpeted hallway, then into another, stark stone hallway, one I recognized.

He wasn't taking me to the duchess. I tried to squirm out of his hands.

'Keep still,' the guard said, tightening his grip. 'Captain wants to talk to you.'

I didn't want to talk to her. Sure as sure, I didn't.

The guard pulled me down the hallway to a door banded with metal; he opened the door and pushed me inside.

Captain Kerrn was there, sitting at a table in what looked like a guards' common room. Swords and pikes stood in racks against the walls, and a long table with benches ran the length of the room. Other guards, including the bristle-bearded Farn, sat around the table, some playing cards, others cleaning weapons or oiling their boots.

They all looked up as we came in. When they saw it was me, they all scowled except for Farn, who stood up and went to stand blocking a door in the opposite wall. Kerrn set down a dagger and a whetstone.

I glanced around the room; the only other way out was through the door we'd come in, and the guard behind me would grab me if I tried to get out that way.

Kerrn got up from her bench, and her ice-chip eyes narrowed as she looked me up and down. 'The duchess is expecting you, so we will keep this short,' Kerrn said in her funny sounding voice with its *sh*'s and gargled *r*'s. 'I have heard a report on you since yesterday. You may have fooled the duchess and those wizards, but I know what you are. You come from the Twilight, and you are a well-known pickpocket and thief.'

'I used to be,' I said, edging away from her. 'But I'm not anymore.'

'You made us look bad,' Kerrn said, 'sneaking into the palace, stealing the duchess's jewel.'

'You made yourselves look bad, not catching me,' I said.

Kerrn came around the table, moving fast. I backed toward the door, but before I got there, Kerrn grabbed me by the front of my coat and bent down to snarl into my face. 'Listen well, thief. Every guard in the city knows what you are and what you have done.' She gave me a shake that made my teeth rattle. 'You put one foot wrong and we will have you.'

She released me and I staggered back, bumping into the guard who had brought me in. All the guards in the room gave me their best menacing looks.

I got the message.

Captain Kerrn turned away. 'Take him out of here.'

The door guard grabbed the back of my coat and hustled me out the door. We quick-walked through the hallways, up the stairs, to the carpeted hallway with the double doors at the end.

My guard knocked at a door, then opened it. Inside, the duchess was sitting behind her desk with a pile of papers before her. As the guard shoved me in, she looked up, removed a pair of spectacles, and raised her eyebrows.

The guard bowed and kept hold of the scruff of my neck.

The duchess rose from behind the desk. 'It's all right, guardsman.' She motioned toward the door. 'You may go.'

'But Your Grace,' the guard protested, 'Captain Kerrn ordered me to watch him until he leaves.'

'Really, guardsman. Go. Call for my advisors to join me shortly.'

'Yes, Your Grace,' the guard said and, with another stiff bow, left the room.

The duchess sat down again. 'Now then. Conn, is it?'

I nodded. I wondered what she thought of me. A thief, as Kerrn thought? A wizard, as I'd shown her the day before?

She gestured gracefully toward a chair, a comfortable one before her desk. 'Won't you sit down?'

I took off my coat and sat down.

She spent a minute examining me, and I returned the favour. I'd really only seen her a few times before, and then I'd been distracted by the call of my locus magicalicus. I could see her resemblance to Rowan. She was tall and slender and had a pale, thin, beautiful face with lines around the eyes and bracketing her mouth. Her red and grey hair was braided and pinned into a crown atop her head. She wore a dark green dress with a green velvet collar and her family crest — tree and leaf — embroidered on each sleeve. Her long fingers were stained with ink, and she wore her spectacles on a gold chain around her neck.

Finished looking me over, she leaned back in her chair. 'Have you my jewel with you?' she asked.

I nodded.

'Mmm.' She looked down her nose at me. 'I see that Nevery has not claimed you.'

What was she talking about?

'You do not wear the winged hourglass, his family crest,' she said.

'I'm Nevery's, if that's what you're asking,' I

said.

'I would not be certain of that if I were you,' she said sharply. 'You'd be wise to be careful. Nevery is dangerous and is not to be trusted, by anyone.'

I wondered what she'd do if I told her Nevery had said the same thing about her.

'Do you know the history of this city, Conn? Does your education go so far?'

'I have hardly any education at all,' I said.

'Mmm. Twenty years ago, in a magical pyrotechnic experiment, Nevery blew up parts of Heartsease and the Dawn Palace. Did you know that?'

I shook my head. I wanted to hear more, but the duchess said, 'Ask your master about it.' She leaned back and pulled a tasselled rope set into the wall. 'Now, you look as if you might like some tea.'

I nodded.

A moment later, the door behind me opened and a servant entered. 'Tea, with biscuits,' the duchess said. The door closed. Her eyes narrowed just a bit. It might have been a smile. 'I hear you like biscuits.'

'I do,' I said. And I was hungry. Maybe she wasn't so bad. She was Rowan's mother, after all.

She leaned her elbows on the desk and rested her chin on her hand. 'You interest me, Conn. My daughter claims you as a friend, and she does not make friends easily.'

The door opened again, and the servant entered on soft feet, bearing a tray of silver tea things and a plate piled high with fluffy biscuits, lightly toasted and dripping with butter. Mmm. The servant put the tray on the duchess's desk, bowed, and silently left the room.

The duchess went on talking while she poured a cup of tea and leaned across the desk to hand it to me. 'I wonder, Conn, about the significance of the fact that the centre jewel from the ducal regalia has turned out to be a locus magicalicus.' From a little pitcher on the tray she added a few drops of milk to her tea. 'You agree that it is significant?'

I nodded, and swallowed down a bite of buttered biscuit. I could guess what she was going to say next. 'And you wonder why me.'

She looked at me over the rim of her cup, her face softened by steam rising from the hot tea. 'Indeed. Why did the finest stone in the ducal regalia come to you?'

'I don't know,' I said. And I didn't. I had to think about it some more.

I took a quick drink of my tea. And I reminded myself to be careful; as Nevery had warned, the duchess was like a puzzle lock. She seemed kind, giving me tea and biscuits, but it didn't mean she was actually kind.

The duchess set down her teacup. 'Well, I think the fact that your locus magicalicus came from my regalia is an indication that my family must reconcile itself to magic. Were you aware, Conn, that years ago it was common for the ruling house of Wellmet to have a court magister, a wizard who was given chambers here in the Dawn Palace? Such a wizard would need to have a strong connection with the ducal house.'

What was she saying, exactly?

'I know your master very well,' she went on. 'Nevery certainly never wanted to take you on as an apprentice. He would be happy to be relieved of your care. I think you would be wise to leave Nevery's damp and drafty old mansion and come live here, in the Dawn Palace.'

Where she could keep an eye on me, she meant. And even though she was mostly right about Nevery – sure as sure, he hadn't wanted me as an apprentice – I wasn't leaving Heartsease. I shook my head.

'Very well,' she said.

I eyed the plate of biscuits. Better not have another one. I needed to ask her the right questions. 'Duchess,' I said. Was that right? Duchess? Or was I supposed to call her something else?

She raised her eyebrows, waiting.

'What d'you think is happening to the magic in Wellmet?' I asked.

She didn't even blink at the change of subject. 'I am told by my advisor that it is a natural ebbing. The problem will eventually reverse itself. I have been assured that the city is not in any danger.'

That didn't make sense. My locus stone was

rare and strange, and it showing up when it had made it clear that something big was happening. 'But you can see that the magic is leaving us, can't you?' I said. 'Without it, the city will die.' I hadn't thought about it that way before, but as I said it aloud I realized that it was true: if the magic died, then Wellmet would die. Soon.

She gave me a level look. 'I am sure you are just repeating Nevery's alarmist ideas.'

'No,' I said, getting frustrated. 'Nevery agrees with you. He doesn't think the city is in danger. But you're both wrong.'

'Really.' She shook her head. 'And what, exactly, do you think is happening?'

'I don't know.'

The duchess, looking past me at the door to her office, repeated, 'I see that you do not. Perhaps my liaison to the magisters can share with you his thoughts on the matter.'

Oh, no. I turned in my chair and, sure enough, Pettivox himself stood in the doorway, tall and broad, his locus magicalicus a thumbnail-shaped gleam of white against his black waistcoat. He strode into the room.

I grabbed my coat and felt in the pocket for my locus stone, but I didn't take it out.

'Well, Magister?' the duchess said.

Pettivox bowed. 'Your Grace.' Without looking at me, he went on. 'What is Nevery's failed apprentice doing here?'

'Going away,' I said, scrambling to my feet. I looked at the duchess. 'Is Pettivox the one who has been telling you not to worry?'

She didn't answer. She didn't have to; I already knew the answer to that question.

As Pettivox turned his glare on me, I edged around him and skiffed out the door. Avoiding the guards, I found my way out of the Dawn Palace to the werelit streets of the Sunrise.

Time to go home to Heartsease. But drats. The duchess would surely tell Pettivox about my locus magicalicus, and Pettivox would tell Crowe. And Nevery was not going to be happy with me.

Headed home from Magisters Hall. Gates through tunnels still on their hinges, assumed boy hadn't returned yet from meeting with the duchess.

At Heartsease, went up to kitchen. No sign of Benet.

Went up to workroom, heard sound of banging from upstairs, attic, where boy has made his lair. Climbed crumbling ladder.

Benet there. Had set a lantern on the floor and by its light was making some kind of frame out of wood. A window frame; he had glass and putty set aside, and a few nails. He nodded as I came up. —Been meaning to get to this, Master, he said.

Attic room freezing. Good man, Benet, thinking of putting glass in the windows.

Looked around at boy's room.

> Nest of holey blankets against the wall
> Pile of books beside it, stacked neatly
> Saucer with stub of candle in it
> Painting of dragon, propped against wall

Arranged on the floor, a collection of junk:
  Burnt scrying globe
  Box of rusted gears
  Stuffed alligator

Examined hearth, peered up chimney, which was blocked with sticks and bird droppings; something had built its nest in there.

—Where is he? Benet asked. With the hammer, he tapped a nail into the corner of the window frame.

—The duchess sent for him, I said.

Benet didn't comment.

Went down to study, stirred up fire, read. Secretary had tabulated notes, as ordered. Did a decent job of it.

Boy came in at last, looking chilled, tired. Went to the fire to warm himself.

—Well, boy? I asked, setting aside papers I was reading.

He was quiet for a moment, thinking. —You were right, Nevery. She's tricky.

—What did she say? I asked.

Boy gave quick grin. —She said you're dangerous and not to be trusted.

Curse the woman, anyway. —What did she want

with you? I asked.

Boy silent again for a few minutes. He sat cross-legged on the hearthstone; the cat came in and climbed into his lap, purring. —Pettivox was there, he said. —He's been advising her about the magical decay.

Not Pettivox again. —Listen, boy, I said. —Pettivox is the duchess's advisor on magical issues. It is his job to keep her informed about the magical decay. Now, what did the duchess want with you?

Boy yawned and rubbed his eyes. —She had one question. Why did her jewel come to me?

Ah. Typical of the duchess, to get straight to the salient point. —And what did you answer? I asked.

—That I don't know.

Expect he doesn't. But if I know boy, it's not for lack of thinking about it. —Anything else? I asked.

—Not really, boy said.

—Well, boy? I said.

He shook his head.

CHAPTER 27

W hen I came down for breakfast the morning after my meeting with the duchess, Nevery and Keeston were sitting at the table, eating, and Benet sat with his chair tilted back against the wall, knitting something with red yarn.

Keeston had, clear as clear, spoken to his master, Pettivox, who had told him about my locus magicalicus. He stared as I stepped into the kitchen, pulling my sweater on over my head and combing my hair with my fingers.

Benet pointed toward the stove, where a warm plate of biscuits and bacon was waiting for me. I hung my scarf and my coat, with my locus magicalicus in the pocket, on a hook beside the door, then fetched my plate and joined them at the table. Keeston watched my every move.

'G'morning, Nevery,' I said, taking a bite of bacon and biscuit.

He glanced up from the book he had open on the table beside his empty plate. 'Hmph,' he said, looking me up and down. 'Benet is right; you do need a haircut.'

'After supper,' Benet said. His knitting needles went *click-tick*.

I ate for a while, thinking, trying to ignore Keeston's fascinated stare. I'd woken up curious about something. 'Nevery,' I said. 'That guard captain from the Dawn Palace. Kerrn?'

Nevery nodded while continuing to read his

book.

'Why does she talk funny?' I asked.

Nevery looked up. 'What do you mean, boy?'

'She said "phlister" like this: *phlishterrrr*.'

'Ah.' Nevery nodded. 'Because she's from Helva, in the far south, beyond the Peninsular Duchies.'

I didn't get it. 'Why would that make her talk funny?'

'Because in Helva they speak Helvan, which leaves that accent when she speaks our language.'

Our language? 'Helvan?' I asked. 'You mean they have different words for everything?'

'Yes, boy,' Nevery said, going back to his book. I could tell what he was thinking: *I don't have time for stupid questions*. But I'd never met anyone before who spoke a different language. Not all that surprising, since most people travelled *away* from Wellmet, not *to* it.

Language. Different words for everything. The new idea washed over me like a wave. 'Magic spells,' I said. Of course!

'What, boy?' Nevery said sharply.

'Magic spells are another language. When we say "*lothfalas*", it means "light" in the language of magic.'

From across the room, my locus magicalicus, responding to the spoken spell, burst into flame, blindingly bright even through the cloth of my coat pocket. Keeston flinched away.

'Put the light out, boy,' Nevery said, blinking. I did.

'Now,' he went on, 'before you make any more wild claims, you must read more magical theory. It has been proven that magical spells are simply a string of linked word parts that focus the wizard's mind so he or she can, with the locus magicalicus, tap into the city's supply of magic and effect the spell.'

I shook my head. 'I don't think so, Nevery. The spells are a language, and we use it to tell the magic what to do.' It made perfect sense.

Nevery was shaking his head, frowning. 'Nonsense. Read Jaspers's essay on the subject, boy, and then tell me what you think.' He snapped his book closed. He started to tell Benet to look for more slowsilver when he went to the marketplace at Sark Square that day.

I didn't listen, eating my biscuit and drinking tea, and thinking about magic and language and magical nodes and Wellmet. If magical spells truly were a language, whose language was it? What, or who, did the spells speak to? Was a magical node not an atmospheric convergence or an upwelling but a living, thinking being?

Oh, Nevery was going to hate this idea. He was going to grumble and tell me to read some treatise and some other book and to stop talking about things I didn't understand.

But I was sure as sure, down in my bones, that I was right about the magic.

'Well, boy?' Nevery said, interrupting my thoughts. I looked up, blinking. He, Benet, and Keeston stood beside the table, waiting for me. I realized that I was sitting with my cup of tea in one hand and the biscuit in the other, staring at the wall.

Nevery shook his head. 'You and Keeston will go to the market with Benet and help him carry the supplies back.'

I nodded and gulped down the rest of my tea

and biscuit. After Keeston had put on his apprentice's robe and I'd put on my coat and wound my scarf around my neck, we went down the stairs and joined Benet, who was dressed warmly and had a truncheon in his belt.

When we stepped out the door, the wind attacked us with icy teeth, tearing at our clothes. Shivering, we crossed the courtyard. In the big tree, the birds hopped up and down on their branches, talking excitedly.

Benet led the way down the tunnel stairs. The tips of Keeston's ears were pink from the cold.

When we got to the gate, we stopped. I waited for Benet to pull out his little grey keystone. But he didn't; he folded his arms and waited, without saying anything.

Keeston glanced nervously at me. 'Don't you want to open it?'

Oh. 'I can do it if you want, but I'm not very good at it.'

'One of you do it,' Benet growled.

Keeston wore his locus magicalicus on its golden chain outside his grey apprentice robe.

Quickly he grabbed it, pointed it toward the lock, closed his eyes – concentrating – and pronounced the opening spell. Nothing happened. He gripped the stone even tighter and tried again. After a sullen moment, the lock turned over and the gate creaked open.

We went on through the damp and chilly tunnels and up the stairs to the Night Bridge.

I glanced aside at Keeston, at his locus stone on its fancy chain. 'You'd better put that away,' I said.

'Why should I?' he said. He was feeling proud of himself for opening the gates, and the sneer had crept back into his voice.

'Why d'you think?' I said.

We stepped from the bridge and into the Twilight. Fleetside Street twisted up the hill before us, covered with packed-down snow and ice, lined on both sides with dirty, broken-down tenement houses and trash; the air smelled of smoke and open cesspits; ragged people watched us from dark doorways.

Quickly Keeston shoved his locus magicalicus on its chain inside the collar of his shirt and buttoned his robe up to his neck.

We started up the hill, trudging into the wind. Benet went first, his hand on the truncheon at his belt, and Keeston and I came behind. I put my head down and shoved my hands into my coat pockets.

Questions and half-thought ideas swirled around in my head. If the spells were the magical being's language, could I learn to speak to it through my locus magicalicus? Would it listen? Could it talk back, tell me what was going on?

I thought back to the question the duchess had asked me the day before: Why had the jewel come to me, a gutterboy and a thief?

Nevery had asked me once about how I had survived the Twilight. I had told him that it was because I had quick hands and I was lucky, and because my mother didn't die until I was old enough to take care of myself. But that didn't really explain it.

Maybe, all along, when I was growing up in the Twilight, the magic of Wellmet had made sure I didn't get sick or end up drudging in a factory or fighting off misery eels in a damp cellar or freezing to death in an alley. The magic had protected me, and when I was ready, it had led me to Nevery, and then to my locus magicalicus.

I knew, sure as sure, why the magic had done all this. It had chosen me. It had saved me so I could save it. I had to do something about the magical decay.

Keeston said something, interrupting my thoughts. 'What?' I said. We were just turning onto Strangle Street, cutting off the worst of the wind. I stepped around an icy pothole.

'I asked you how you dare talk to your master like that,' Keeston said.

'Like what?' I knew Keeston didn't like me calling Nevery by his right name, but we'd already been through that.

'You interrupted him reading and he snapped at you, but you weren't afraid, and then you contradicted him. "I don't think so, Nevery," you said.' He swallowed. 'If I'd said that to Magister Pettivox, he would have beaten me until my bones ached.'

I shrugged. 'Nevery wouldn't.'

'How do you know?' Keeston looked truly interested. 'Everybody's terrified of Magister Nevery, even the other magisters. He's got this' – he lowered his voice – 'this brutal mercenary bodyguard working for him. And he was banished for blowing up his mansion, and he's very fierce.' He shivered.

'He just wouldn't.' I shrugged. 'Not me, and not you, either.'

Keeston shook his head.

'And Benet's not so bad,' I added.

A pace ahead of us, Benet looked over his shoulder and snorted.

And then we were attacked.

Completed gauge to measure magical level last night, made some initial measurements. Findings not entirely unexpected. Magic level in Wellmet is no longer decaying. Level is absolutely steady, unchanging. But very, very low. Dangerously so.

Reread Micnu's treatise. Low magical levels could be related to extreme cold; the node Wellmet is built upon could simply be frozen, and once the thaws of spring arrive, magic will begin to flow again.

Yet Arhionvar is an example that must not be ignored.

May propose to magisters that we reduce use of magic until spring thaws.

CHAPTER 28

Benet, Keeston, and I turned off Strangle Street into an alley that would take us to Sark Square, when four burly men loomed up before us. Minions, I realized; they had that oversized, mean-eyed look, and they carried clubs and knives. Drats. I'd been stupid. Crowe had always had a word out on me, and now that I had the jewel locus magicalicus, he'd want me for himself more than he ever had. He must have every minion in the Twilight on the lookout.

Benet stopped, Keeston and I behind him. 'Run,' he said quietly.

Not likely. I looked over my shoulder. My heart jolted with fright. Two more minions stepped across the mouth of the alley; we were trapped. 'Two more behind us, Benet,' I said.

He cursed and pulled his truncheon out of his belt.

All at the same time, the six minions closed in around us. Benet stepped forward and, ducking a swung club, bashed one of them in the jaw; another minion shoved Keeston to the snowy ground, and four of them grabbed me. I struggled as hard as I could, kicking and biting and trying to twist out of their grip, but they were too strong. 'Benet!' I shouted as the minions started dragging me out of the alley. One of them clapped a hand over my mouth; I bit him and he cursed and cuffed me on the side of the head.

Roaring, Benet bulled through the two minions he was fighting and punched in the face one of the minions holding me. I wriggled out of a minion's grip, but another one grabbed my arm.

Keeston sat on the ground where he'd been pushed, staring at the fight, his mouth and eyes wide. 'Do some magic!' I shouted at him, elbowing a minion in the nose. Keeston pulled his locus stone from inside his robe and held it in shaking hands. 'Do it!' I shouted again.

'I c-can't remember any spells,' he squeaked. One of the minions rounded on him, and he shrieked and scuttled backward into a snowdrift, away from the fight.

Benet cracked his truncheon across the hand of the minion holding me, and I wrenched myself away, groping in my pocket for my locus magicalicus. 'Benet, cover your eyes!' I yelled, and as he threw his arm across his face, I shouted, *Lothfalas!*

As I pulled the stone from my pocket, the magic surged through it and blazed, white-bright and blinding, filling the alley with a wave of light. The minions flinched away. I put the light out and shoved the stone back into my pocket. 'Clear,' I gasped, and while the minions blinked the brights from their eyes, Benet bashed one of them on the head and turned to grapple with another.

The one I'd elbowed wiped blood from his nose, pushed me aside, and, pulling a knife from his belt, slashed at Benet's arm. Benet grunted in pain. Panting, we backed away from the three minions left; two of the ones Benet had bashed were just getting to their feet, and another lay on the ground, moaning. The snowy ground was spattered with droplets of blood.

'Get 'em,' one of the minions said grimly, wiping blood from his face, and they were on us again.

Benet swung his truncheon, connecting with a *crack crack crack*. His other fist was a hammer, and the minions were nails. A minion stumbled past me, blood fountaining from his nose. Another fell to the ground, groaning. But still, the others kept coming.

I only knew one other spell, and I didn't want to use it. But I had no choice. Darting behind Benet, I clenched my hand around my locus magicalicus, chanting the embero. *Tumbriltumbrilu-lartambe* ... One of the minions came after me and I dodged him, slipping in the snow, still reciting the spell. Then a cudgel whooshed through the air before me, missing Benet and striking me a crashing blow on my chest. I gasped for breath, fell to my knees, and continued the spell. *Please, magic,* I thought, still pant-chanting. *Don't turn Benet into a bear, because he hates it. And not Keeston, either. Just the minions, please.*

With the last of my breath, I finished the spell — *lilotarkolilotar-kennan!*

With a crackle of blue sparks, the embero spell exploded across the alleyway, flinging me back against a brick wall, then to the icy cobblestones. As the spell struck, the air cracked apart where the minions had stood, then slammed back together with a muffled *boom*. Blue sparks danced in a whirlwind. Four clubs and a knife clattered to the ground.

Where the minions had stood were three rats with scaly, naked tails, a rooster, a black snake, and a little hairy man with a long tail, shivering and looking dazedly around. One of the rats snarled and leaped at Benet's foot; he kicked it and it squealed and skittered off down the alley. The others followed.

Across the alley Benet, himself unchanged, leaned against the wall, holding his ribs with one arm, the other arm dangling at his side. Blood dripped from his fingertips onto the snow. Keeston stood gripping his locus stone with both hands, staring at the black snake, which was slithering after the other animals.

'I'm sorry,' I said, climbing to my feet, aching in my bones. 'It's the only spell I know.'

'It'll do,' Benet said. He nodded in the direction the rats and other animals had gone. 'More where they came from.'

We needed to go, to get out of the Twilight. Benet, wincing, glanced at the slash on his arm, then gripped it with his other hand to stop the blood. 'Come on,' he growled.

We headed down the hill, the wind behind us, to the Night Bridge, then down the steps to the secret tunnel to the islands. I tried to walk carefully, because my ribs ached with every step; my face throbbed where a minion had hit me. Finally we reached the first gate, where I pulled out my locus stone and spoke the opening spell. The gate flash-crashed open; Benet shoved his booted foot in the way to stop the gate slamming closed again.

Keeston's eyes grew wider as we blasted through the rest of the gates to Heartsease. When we went through the last gate, I said to him, 'Run and tell Nevery we're coming,' and without even hesitating he dashed away.

At the bottom of the stairs, Benet paused. His face looked green, and blood seeped between his fingers. I waited with him until he nodded, and we went up the stairs.

Was writing up conclusions about magical decay.

Heard door downstairs slam open; secretary dashed up the stairs into study, eyes wide, panting. Said they'd been attacked in the Twilight.

As they came up stairs, boy looked well enough, but Benet's arm wounded, dripping blood; had his hand on boy's shoulder, steadying himself.

Cleaned and bandaged nasty gash on Benet's arm, checked egg-sized bump on the side of his head. He shook me off, pointed at the boy.

—He got clubbed, Benet said. —Ribs.

Boy protested, but got him to take off his sweater and shirt. Had nasty, seeping bruise the size of a saucer, but rib bones not cracked or broken. While he got dressed again, brewed tea, added painkilling herbs and gave them each a cup.

Not a mark on secretary, from what I could see.

CHAPTER 29

'**B**enet,' I said the next day.
'Keep still,' Benet said. He
was cutting my hair with
scissors. I sat on a stool in the middle
of the kitchen, and Keeston was at
the table with a pile of papers
Nevery had set him to reading.

'What d'you think
happened in the fight?' I
asked. I thought I knew, but
I wanted to see if Benet
thought so, too.

'Got the fluff beat out of us,'

Benet said. 'You did magic, we got out of there.'

I nodded.

'Keep still, you,' Benet said again. He snipped for a while.

'Not too short,' I said. *Snip snip snip.* 'Benet, I think those minions were after me.'

'Hmph,' Benet said. 'Think so?'

'Do *you* think so?' I asked.

'Yes.'

From the table, Keeston looked up from his papers. 'I think they were after you, too, um, Conn.'

Benet growled. He was still angry that Keeston hadn't helped us fight off the minions.

Keeston trembled under Benet's glare. 'T-two of them went after Benet. Four tried to grab you, Conn, and they ignored me.'

I nodded. That's how I remembered it, too.

And I remembered, with a little jolt, that Keeston was probably reporting everything he saw and heard to his master, Pettivox. Drats. I had been starting to like Keeston.

Well, I'd just have to watch what I said around him.

So the minions had been after me; even Keeston agreed. Nevery wouldn't believe it. But the attack was one more reason to be sure as sure of two things. One, that Pettivox had told Crowe about my locus magicalicus, and two, that Crowe thought I was a threat to his plans, whatever they were, and was trying harder than he ever had before to pick me up off the streets.

I had to find out what they were up to. And now that I knew the Underlord's minions were looking for me, I'd have to be very careful every time I left Heartsease.

'It's a little lopsided,' Keeston said.

Benet and I turned to stare at him.

He pointed at me. 'The haircut. It's longer on the left side than the right.'

Benet growled at him and he flinched and went back to his papers.

Then Benet cut the left side shorter.

Later that day, I was reading in Nevery's study, books piled on the table all around me. Nevery had told me to read a treatise about some lost city, but I couldn't be bothered. I wanted to find out if any other wizards had written about magic spells.

Keeston sat at the other end of the table, collating more of Nevery's notes. Nevery himself was at Magisters Hall preparing to present his conclusions about the magical decay – I wasn't sure what he would tell them.

The air outside was perishing cold. The tall windows were covered with ice crystals and the wind howled around the outside of the mansion. Despite Keeston's company, I felt desolate and empty inside. The magic had faded; I couldn't feel its warm presence anywhere. I kept shivering and wrapping myself in more blankets.

Hearing Benet come up the stairs, I looked up from my book. He came into the room, followed by Rowan.

'Hello, Ro,' I said.

Keeston jumped to his feet. 'Lady Rowan!'

'Hello, Keeston, Conn.' She took off her coat and student's robe and her scarf and went to the fire to warm her hands. 'I had a few guards row me over. The river is freezing,' she said. 'I don't know how much colder it can get.'

She hadn't come to talk about the weather. I closed my book, shed my blankets, and got carefully to my feet. I was still sore from getting bashed in the ribs and had a bruise on the side of my face. She raised her eyebrows. 'I suppose you're going to tell me what happened to you.'

'D'you want to see the attic?' I said.

'Oh, more than anything,' she said brightly. Keeston made a move, as if he might come with us, but she said, 'I'm sorry to have interrupted your work, Keeston. Do continue. We'll be back in a few minutes.'

We went out together and up the stairs to the fourth floor, then scrambled up the ladder to the attic.

'Your room?' Rowan asked.

I nodded and handed her a blanket. I wrapped myself in a blanket and sat on the floor with my back against the wall, where she joined me.

'So?' she asked.

'Benet and I were attacked in the Twilight,' I said. 'We're all right.'

'Indeed.'

We sat in silence for a few minutes.

'What's going on?' she asked.

I shrugged.

'Something's going on,' she muttered.

'What?' I asked.

She looked up at the sloped ceiling. 'My mother meets every day with that nasty magister, Pettivox.'

I perked up at that. 'D'you know what they talk about?'

Rowan gave me her glinting sideways glance. 'Are you asking, Connwaer, if I spy on my own mother?'

Well, yes. I nodded.

'Mmm.' She huddled her blanket up around her shoulders. 'It's cold in here. Freezing.'

It wasn't so bad. Better since Nevery had asked Benet to put in windowpanes. I waited.

'I think Pettivox is watching her,' Rowan said. 'To see what she's going to do, or maybe to keep her from doing anything. My mother is not stupid, Conn. She knows something is going on.'

I nodded.

'Well?' she said, impatient. 'What is it? Somehow I feel certain that you are at the centre of it, whatever it is. And I assume it has something to do with your latest black eye.'

I took a deep breath and thought about it for a minute. I couldn't be sure her mother wasn't working with Pettivox and the Underlord. But I knew I could trust Rowan. 'Ro, what d'you think the magic is?' I asked. She'd had apprentice classes, so she must have thought about it.

'Well . . .' She looked at me, then away. 'I've always heard that magic is dangerous. I'm studying magic so that I'll know what kind of regulations are needed for the city to be safe.' She shivered and wrapped herself more tightly in the blanket. 'I've read Micnu and Carron on magical nodes, of course. I suppose magic is something like what they say it is, a natural force that gathers in one place.'

'No,' I said. 'It's not. Magic is a living being. And Wellmet's magic, the being' – I shook my head – 'it's in danger.'

Rowan stared at me, eyes wide.

I went on quickly. 'The magic chose me to find the leaf jewel.' I reached under the blanket and into my pocket and pulled out my locus magicalicus. It glowed spring green in the dust-dim room. 'I'm the one who's supposed to help it.'

'Help it? This magic being?' Rowan asked. She shook her head.

'To save it.'

She shifted a little away from me and looked me over, her eyebrows raised.

She didn't believe me. But I might as well tell her the rest of it, anyway. 'Nevery thinks the magical level is just ebbing, but I think the Underlord is doing something to the magic. I've seen Pettivox at Dusk House and in the Twilight, which means Pettivox is helping Underlord Crowe. I have to figure out what they're doing and how to stop them.'

'Mmm-hmmm,' Rowan said.

'Yes,' I said. Drats, I didn't want her to tell me I was being stupid. We sat without talking for a few minutes. The room had gotten so cold that I could see my breath in the air. Outside the frosted-over windows, the sky was darkening.

'Pettivox asked my mother about you,' she said at last.

Not surprising. The duchess had probably told him all about the thief who'd stolen the largest jewel from her necklace.

Rowan gave me a sharp half-grin. 'She told him that she asked you to serve as the ducal magister.'

She had, sort of. I shrugged.

'Connwaer,' Rowan said, impatient. 'My mother, who hates magic, asked you' — she pointed at me — 'the very young, former thief, apprentice of her worst enemy, to be her magister. I told you she's not stupid. She knows something is going on and she knows you're involved.'

Oh. Well, good. 'D'you believe me about the magical being?'

She shook her head. 'I don't know. It's a — well, it's typical of you, isn't it? It's a very strange idea. I have to think about it.'

All right.

'What are you going to do?' Rowan asked.

I wasn't sure. But I couldn't stay here and

wait for something to happen. When he got back, I would have to convince Nevery that it was time for us to go out into the city, to find out what was really going on.

Preparing to present findings tonight to magisters. Notes collated, precedents listed, charts drawn up. Yet am uncertain about conclusions. Magic level remains extremely low.

Find there has been corresponding fall in temperature. Weather worsening. Coldest I've ever seen it; river frozen almost all the way across.

Yet cold weather is not enough to explain such calculated drops in magic level. Not sure the magical decay is natural.

CHAPTER 30

Despite the new windows, the air in my attic was freezing. An icy draft blew down the chimney and swirled around the room. Even wrapped up in my blankets and all my clothes, I was too cold and empty to sleep.

Finally, I took my blankets and went down to sleep in the study, on the hearth.

In the middle of the night I woke up to Nevery standing over me, nudging me with his foot. It reminded me of my first day as an apprentice – though I hadn't really become Nevery's apprentice until later. It seemed like a long time ago.

Nevery took off his hat and cloak and flung them on a chair. Then he stepped around me and flung a shovelful of coal onto the fire, which snapped and hissed as it flared up.

I yawned and sat up, my blankets still wrapped around me, and leaned against the wall beside the fireplace. He must have just returned from the meeting at Magisters Hall. From the looks of it, the meeting hadn't gone well. 'What did you tell the magisters?' I asked.

Nevery paced to his chair and, shoving his hat and cloak out of the way, sat down. 'Interesting that you should ask that, boy. If I told you about the meeting, who would you report to?'

I blinked. 'Nobody.' I unwrapped myself from my blankets and climbed stiffly to my feet.

'I have realized, boy, why you are so keen to

convince me that Pettivox is involved with the Underlord.'

'Because he *is* involved with the Underlord.'

Nevery looked angry, his brows drawn, frowning down. 'At the meeting, Pettivox told me of something I should have realized before.'

Oh, no. A feeling of dread started to gather in my stomach.

'First,' Nevery said, 'Pettivox admitted that he has been going to the Twilight. But that is because he is the magister assigned as liaison to the duchess, and the duchess sent him to keep an eye on the Underlord. And he told me something else.'

The room was silent for a long moment. In the fireplace, little flames licked over the pile of coal; outside, the wind moaned.

'Your name,' Nevery said, finally. 'It is a true name.'

I nodded. *Connwaer*. It made me think of black feathers and bright, yellow eyes.

'Crowe. Also a true name.'

The feeling of dread spread from my stomach and down my legs and arms, and I started to shake. 'Nevery,' I said, and my voice was shaking, too.

Scowling, Nevery got up from his chair. 'Pettivox told me that long ago Crowe identified you, his *nephew*, as his successor, that you lived in Crowe's house and were trained by him in spying and sneaking. Can you deny it?'

I shook my head. No, I couldn't.

Nevery scowled and jabbed his finger toward the door. 'Get out. You are no apprentice of mine.'

'Yes I am,' I said, clenching my fists.

'Out!' he roared.

I went out, slamming the door behind me.

Heading down the dark stairway, I realized that my knees were shaking, so I sat down on a step and put my head in my hands.

So Nevery had finally realized that the Underlord and I shared a true, family name. That was enough for Pettivox to convince him that I was a liar and spy. I hadn't been Crowe's for a long time, but Nevery would never believe that. Meanwhile, Nevery and the other wizards were going to study the situation and wait for the magical levels to improve. But that wasn't going to happen. I had a feeling that things would get worse very soon.

Hearing footsteps, I looked up. Somehow, tears had gotten onto my cheeks, so I wiped them quickly away.

Benet was coming up the stairs, carrying a tray and candle. 'What,' he said.

I shifted aside so he could get past. But he stopped a few steps below me, waiting.

I wasn't sure what to tell him. I trusted Benet completely, but he was Nevery's man.

'I have to go out for a while,' I said. Nevery wouldn't believe anything I said, so I would find proof. I could get into the Underlord's mansion. Crowe and Pettivox were up to something there. If I spied on them, I'd have the proof I needed.

'Out?' Benet said. 'Into the city?'

I nodded.

Benet glared. 'Don't be stupid, you.'

'I'll be careful,' I said.

Benet shook his head and went on up the stairs.

When I used my locus stone to go through the tunnel gate, the magic arced into the lock and sputtered, and the gate creaked open and stayed open. No sparks, no crashing and slamming.

In the dark tunnel, I inspected my locus magicalicus. Its glow seemed dimmer than usual. The magical level must have dropped very low. The night felt empty, and colder than ever. I didn't have much time.

The streets of the Twilight were dark and deserted. A freezing wind shrieked down the steep, empty streets, driving snow before it. The factories by the river were silent and still. As I crept through the cramped, twisty back alleys, closer to Dusk House, I kept my eyes and ears open but saw nothing, heard nothing, just the wind.

Finally I was close enough. I found a dead-end alley piled with trash and slick with ice; in the corner farthest from the street, I knelt down and dug a little cave in a dirty snowbank. The freezing air bit at my bare fingers as I pulled my locus magicalicus from my pocket and placed it into the little cave.

Then, after checking that the alley was still empty, I put my hand on the jewel and whispered the embero.

The spell seeped out of my locus magicalicus

and crept into my hand. With a *pop*, everything went black.

I opened my eyes; the alley had grown large. I got shakily to my four feet, the icy cobblestones cold under my paws. The wind ruffled my fur. I checked on my locus magicalicus. The spell had melted the snow around it, and it sat in a little puddle of water that was quickly turning to ice. With a paw I patted it, then headed out of the alley, toward the Underlord's mansion.

Confronted boy with his perfidy; he has run away. Expected it. Reporting to Crowe, no doubt, that he has been found out.

Didn't want apprentice in the first place. Should have remembered from the start what he is — thief. Liar and spy. Stupid of me to forget that. Curse him.

CHAPTER 31

Blending with the night, I slunk through the alleys until I arrived at Dusk House. Even though it was the middle of the night, the barred windows were bright with lights. The air felt like it was full of invisible needles; it pulsed and hummed and made my fur stand up on end. Something was going on in there, sure as sure.

I padded up to the gate and slid through the bars, then went down the edge of the gravelled drive and around the back of the mansion, where I found a cluster of sheds and a small, dirty courtyard. A door opened and closed, and I heard footsteps crunching across the frozen snow. Another door creaked; somebody visiting a privy, I guessed. I slunk closer. When the person – a minion with a knife in his belt – crunched toward the back door again, I followed him inside. He didn't notice me.

I headed down the dark corridors, slinking through open doors, glad for my black fur, which kept me hidden in the shadows, until I came to the room with the bookcase and the stairway, the room where I'd seen Pettivox when I'd spied during Nevery's visit. The room was empty, the bookcase propped open. Behind it loomed the dark doorway.

I padded across the room to the top of the narrow, dark stairs. I paused at the opening. My whiskers twitched; I smelled something bad, something wrong. If I really were a cat, I might have known what it was, but all I knew was that the smell made my tail bristle and put my ears back.

But I had to get down the stairs. I crouched on the edge of the step, my tail twitching, and peeked over. Nothing but darkness. I hopped down three steps and paused. From below, I heard clanking and the scrape of gears. Men shouted. The air pulsed. Then came a roar, like wind and thunder in the middle of a storm, and then a *crack* like lightning striking. My paws trembled against the stone steps. What were they doing down there? I had to go on, to find out. I jumped down a few more steps and peered into the darkness below.

Two red points of light, low to the ground, looked back at me. All my fur stood on end. I went down another step.

From out of the gloom, dragging itself up the stairs, came an enormous rat, bigger than I was, with a scaly, naked tail, ragged grey fur, and sharp teeth. The rat lowered its head and hissed. Its red eyes gleamed.

It was a minion, I realized; one of the

Underlord's men who had attacked Benet and me in the alley. Did it know who I was, that I had changed it from a man into a rat?

The rat climbed up another step until it was just below me. Then, in a whirl of snarl and lashing tail, it leaped.

As it came at me, its teeth bared, I rolled onto my back and raised my four clawed paws. We tangled together, slash-gnashing, and bumped down two steps. I swiped a paw across its snout and it lunged at me, hissing. I darted out of its way, landing on four paws, crouched growling, my tail whipping back and forth.

It came at me again, slashing at my side with its sharp teeth, but I ducked past it and sank my own teeth deep into its tail – it tasted terrible. The rat whirled to rake me with its claws. I spat out its tail, leaped onto its back, and swiped my claws across its red eyes, then I sprang off. Squealing, shaking its head, the rat backed away, blinded.

Watching it carefully, I eased away. It crouched on the step, pawing at its eyes, hissing. Quietly, I hopped down a step, then another.

My fur settled and I went on down the steps to the first turning. I looked back, but the rat had not followed. I slunk around the corner, then down to the second turning in the stairway. The sound of clanking and gears had gotten louder, almost deafening. I sat on the step and peered around the corner.

Like when I'd been here before, I saw a huge, bright space, men, glinting metal gears. I pulled my head back and blinked, then looked again, more carefully.

The workroom, which was huge and cavernous, had been dug out of the rock. It was lit with flickering werelights set along the rock walls and hanging from the ceiling. I saw men hunched over papers – diagrams or plans – at a long table, and other men wrestling with a fat, pulsing hose. Along the edge of the room were more tables covered with glass jars and vials and copper odds and ends, tubes and wires and boxes of screws.

And in the middle of the workroom, taking up most of the space, looming up to the ceiling, squatted a huge, sprawling, gleaming geared device. Its middle was a huge tank, stitched across with rivets and bristling with tubes and dials. On one side it had a series of gears, gnashing together; on the other were copper coils, swollen hoses, and crystal tubes dripping with slowsilver. The device pulsed and heaved.

As I watched, a long piston near the floor groaned forward and an immense gear turned; the men shouted, steam hissed out in smoky clouds, and there came a crush-rushing of wind, of *something* being sucked in toward the device. A vent in the side gaped. Gears shrieked, thunder crashed, and the lights went out, and deep inside I felt a sudden empty, lonely ache.

The lights flickered on. A few men went to the machine to check the dials; other men went back to looking at the diagrams. The air settled and the machine hummed.

I backed away from the turning and went up a few steps. Then I crouched down, shivering. In the darkness, on the step, I realized what they were doing. They were sucking in all of Wellmet's magic and storing it. The device was a capacitor, like the melted machine I'd found in

Heartsease, but huge. A prison for the magic. What would they do with the magic, once they had it all? Would they kill it?

I licked my paw and washed it across my face and whiskers. Enough worrying. I had the proof I needed; now I had to get out, change myself back into a boy, and tell somebody what was going on. It wasn't too late.

I raced up the stairs, past the place where I'd fought the rat. After reaching the top of the stairs, I got halfway across the room before I realized that I was surrounded.

The rat, its snout bloody and its teeth bared, was waiting for me, and it had brought help: two more rats.

Three against one. Not a fight I could win. I didn't pause, just leaped for the door. Squealing, the rats scrabbled and leaped after me.

I pelted down a hallway, skidded around a corner, and found myself faced with three closed doors, a dead end. The rats swirled 'round the corner and stopped. Snarling, they paced closer, lashing their tails. One of the rats bared its fangs and then leaped forward; at the same time, the other rats swarmed over me, biting. I bit back, and clawed, and squirmed away as teeth slashed my foreleg. I rolled onto my paws and darted away.

I raced down the corridors and around corners, the rats right behind me, until I got to the main entryway. My paws skidded on the slick stone floor as I raced for the front door.

A minion was coming in, just closing the door; he stared as I raced toward him and darted between his legs and outside, into the cold, dark night. Behind me, the door slammed, closing the rats inside.

I tumbled to the bottom of the front steps and crouched on the freezing ground, shivering, trying to catch my breath. The slash on my front leg burned, and I had rat bites on my back and sides. Limping, I crept away into the night.

Stayed up late monitoring magical level with gauge. Several times, level fell abruptly. Alarmed. Almost no magic left in city.

Went to study to check notes. Read until early morning. No new conclusions. Tired. Benet came up with tea.

—Conn isn't back yet, sir, Benet said.

Told him cursed boy isn't coming back at all. Benet asked why. Told him boy is spy for Underlord.

—No he isn't, Master, Benet said.

Told him I had proof: boy and Underlord share a family name.

Benet looked interested. —Do they? Then he shrugged. —Still, Conn's not a spy for Crowe.

—How do you know? I asked.

—He wouldn't, Benet said. He stood in doorway with arms folded. Seemed very certain. —Sir, when we were attacked in the Twilight, it was Crowe's men.

They were after Conn.

Why would Crowe send men to attack his own spy? Not sure what to think.

CHAPTER 32

I went straight back to the dark alleyway where my locus magicalicus was hidden. The cave of ice had frozen around it, so I had to paw it out of the snow onto the ground. Then I put my front paws on it and thought the

reversed embero spell.

In the darkness, my locus stone gave a feeble glow; almost all the magical being was imprisoned in the Underlord's device. I thought through the reverse embero again. Slowly, I changed back, part of me cat, part of me boy. I said the spell over and over again until every claw and whisker had disappeared. And the tail.

When I looked up, morning had come. On my arm was a long, bloody gash from one of the rats' teeth. It stung, but it hadn't bled much. Stiff from crouching, I got to my feet and put my locus magicalicus in my coat pocket. Overhead, clouds hung low and grey, and flecks of snow blew down the street beyond the alley. I peered around the corner. Nobody was about.

I wasn't sure what to do. The best thing would be to go to Nevery and try to convince him that I'd seen the device. But Nevery . . .

I took a shuddery breath. Nevery was furious with me, and he wouldn't believe anything I told him. I didn't have time to argue with him.

I could try going to Brumbee. But what could he do? He'd wring his hands and worry, and then he'd call a meeting of the magisters. And besides, Pettivox had told the other magisters that I was Crowe's spy. Drats.

Then I remembered what Rowan had told me. Her mother, the duchess, was clever. She knew something was going on. I had a feeling she would listen to me if I told her about the Underlord's device.

That decided, I headed for the Dawn Palace.

I ran as fast as I could from the Twilight, across the Night Bridge, and up the hill toward the Dawn Palace, stopping now and then to catch my breath, then running again.

It was early morning and barely light, and the streets were deserted. Too quiet. The magic level had gotten so low, even people who weren't wizards could feel it, and they'd shut themselves up inside their snug houses, frightened of what was happening outside.

Finally I got to the Dawn Palace. As I crunched down the icy driveway, my breath steaming in the air, the two guards on duty at the main doors caught sight of me.

One of them was Farn, the guard from the cells, the one who had given me the phlister.

He started down the steps toward me.

I stopped.

Farn called over his shoulder to the other guard. 'Tell Captain Kerrn that the wizard's thief is here.' He ran a few steps, then reached out to grab me.

The duchess wasn't expecting me this time, I realized. Curse it, Kerrn had warned me not to come back, or she'd throw me in the cells again. She'd chain me up and force me to drink phlister. She sure as sure wouldn't let me talk to the duchess.

I ducked under Farn's reaching hand. He lunged after me, slipped on the ice, and fell. 'Come back here, you,' he grunted, getting to his feet. Two more guards burst out of the front door of the palace and hurried down the stairs.

I backed away. 'Tell the duchess to send men to the Twilight,' I shouted. 'The Underlord is stealing Wellmet's magic!'

I didn't have time for more. Farn lurched after me again and the other guards reached the bottom of the steps.

They chased me out the front gate and down the hill, shouting. One of them split off from the others to cut down another street.

I pelted down the hill as fast as I could. Went 'round corners, down alleyways, still heard the shouting. They had plenty of men to call on, and they knew this part of the city better than I did.

Finally I got clear and ducked into a cellar coal hole. Trying to catch my breath, I crouched in the darkness. My legs quivered with tiredness from all the running. Outside, the chase faded into the distance.

After a while, I climbed up out of the coal hole and into a deserted alleyway. I had to get back to Heartsease. Maybe Nevery would listen. Keeping my head down and my scarf wrapped around my face, I eased along a street of closed-up shops. I turned a corner, and someone grabbed me and yanked a black bag down over my head.

Trying to work. Distracted. Benet so certain that boy not a spy. Benet a good man, not easily fooled.

Decided to try scrying for boy. Expected to see him with Crowe.

Scrying globes sensitive to presence of magic. Boy's locus magicalicus, magical abilities, should make him appear bright as a shooting star against a night sky within scrying globe. Polished largest globe with wormsilk cloth, set it in bowl of warm water, said anstriker spell.

Nothing. Not enough ambient magic for spell to effect. Scrying globe stayed dark, useless.

CHAPTER 33

Captured. Not by Kerrn's men, though. They weren't black bag types.

I struggled, but the men who'd jumped me gave me a couple of thumps, wrapped a rope tightly around the bag, then one threw me over his shoulder. I tried shouting, but the bag muffled my voice. And the streets were empty, so nobody would hear.

They went quickly through the streets,

me with my head hanging down, bumping up and down in the bag. It was completely dark and the cloth pressed up against my face smelled moldy and a little like rotten potatoes.

The one carrying me paused for a moment, then stepped up. I heard the sound of a door opening and then closing.

'Want me to take him?' a deep voice said.

The man carrying me answered. 'Nah. Doesn't weigh anything.'

'He'll be here in a moment,' another voice said.

They stood around waiting. I tried wriggling, and the man carrying me set me on my feet, but kept a tight grip on my shoulders.

Someone else came into the room. He walked with a heavy tread. Silence. Inside the bag, I felt prickly, like somebody was looking me over.

'Are you sure it's him?' he said. Pettivox. I recognized his high-pitched voice at once.

'Yes, sir,' one of his men answered. 'The lockpick. Underlord's had a word out on him. We know him.'

'Good. He will be very pleased.' Pettivox paused for a moment. 'I think we shall put him in one of the storage rooms, downstairs. He will want to have a look at him later. Don't let him get away; he's slippery.'

Who was 'he'? Underlord Crowe? That was someone I definitely didn't want to see. I wrenched myself out of the man's grip. But the rope was wrapped too tightly around me, so all I did was topple over. One of the men laughed.

They picked me up again and carried me down some stairs, then along an echoing corridor. They unwrapped the ropes, pulled off the bag, and before I could find my feet, they shoved me into a dark place. The door slammed behind me and locked.

After a moment catching my breath, I picked myself off the floor, pulled my lockpick wires out of my pocket, and felt over the door for the keyhole. Found it. It was gritty, maybe rusty. Still, if a key could open it, so could I. Just as I was probing the lock with the wires, I heard the scrape of a boot on stone. A guard was stationed outside the door.

I put the wires back into my pocket. The

room was completely dark, without a glimmer of light. I paced across it with my hands raised until I got to a wall. I felt in my pocket for my locus magicalicus and brought it out; it glowed very faintly, a soft-edged bit of dawn in my hand. The light wasn't enough to see much by.

The room was small, maybe three paces across. Low ceiling, no windows. The walls were clammy stone that radiated cold. Not the kind of biting cold that takes your breath away, but the kind of damp cold that seeps down into your bones and makes you miserable.

For hours I paced, gripping my locus magicalicus, pausing once in a while to listen at the door for the guard. I had to get out. The magic was in trouble; if Pettivox and the Underlord were going to do anything, they were going to do it *soon*.

I bounced off one wall and whirled to pace, *step step step* across the cell to the door. Outside, two deep voices were talking. Then, right at the door, I heard the jingling of keys in the lock.

I backed away from the door, a hand in my coat pocket holding my locus stone, and put my back against the cold, clammy wall. The door cracked open, swung wide. A dark shadow stepped into the cell.

Click-tick. Click-tick-tick.

A minion came up behind the shadow and opened a lantern.

I put up my hand to shield my eyes. When I blinked the brights away, I saw him as he stepped closer.

Underlord Crowe.

He looked just the same as he always had. Ordinary. Not tall, not short; not handsome, not plain; not old, not young. Neat black suit, cloak with a fur collar. Combed and oiled dark hair. Pale grey eyes like locks, like grey locks with a keyhole in the middle showing only emptiness. He looked me over and his face stayed still and blank.

He had a hand in his cloak pocket, where he kept his clicker device.

The cold from the wall seeped through my clothes and into my bones. I shivered.

'You. Connwaer,' he said, his voice flat.

I nodded.

Without taking his gaze from me, he spoke to one of the minions in the doorway. 'Has he been searched for lockpick wires?'

'Ah, no, sir,' said the minion. He shifted, and the lantern light wavered across the damp cell walls.

'See that it is done,' Crowe said. 'Check his hair, the collar of his shirt, his boots, and the seams of his clothing. Do not touch the locus magicalicus when you search him.'

'Yes, sir,' the minion said.

Crowe nodded. A silent, dark moment. 'Your locus magicalicus, I am told, is exceptional,' Crowe said. 'And my man Pettivox says you have shown an interest in our affairs. Not very intelligent of you, was it, to draw my notice when you have tried for so long to avoid it.'

I stayed quiet. I wasn't going to talk to him at all if I could help it.

'Your new skills make you worth even more to me.'

I didn't answer.

'You are just as stubborn as you ever were.' He paused. *Click-tick*. 'You will not join me; that is clear enough. So it follows that you must be dealt with.' Crowe shifted a little, and I edged away from him, along the cold, dank wall, into the corner of the tiny stone room. 'We will not seek to harm you. You will simply be left here.' *Click-tick-tick-tick*, *tick-tick*. 'Four days, possibly five depending on the variables. And you will cease to trouble my plans, just as your mother did.' The way he said it wasn't a threat, he was just informing me of what would be. He was completely cold, colder than the iciest wind off the river. He looked me up and down; his keyhole eyes calculated how much I was worth, which was nothing.

He turned on his heel, his cloak flaring around. 'See to it,' he said to the minions, and left.

The minion holding the lantern set it down in the doorway and crowded into the cell, with the other minion right behind him, blocking the door. 'Now, keep still,' one of them said. He reached out for me, and I ducked under his hands, pulling out my locus magicalicus.

'Watch the stone!' one of the minions shouted; the other one grabbed me by the collar of my coat and slammed me hard against the wall; I lost my grip, and my locus stone flew from my hand and went clattering across the stone floor. Before I could go after it, the minion put his forearm across my throat. I gasped for breath. 'Keep still,' he growled. I kept still.

While he held me against the wall, the other one searched me. He found the lockpick wires in my pocket right away. 'Keep looking,' the minion holding me said. He loomed over me, breathing stinking breath down into my face while the other minion checked my shirt collar, ran his fingers through my hair, pulled my boots off and checked them, and finally found the other set of lockpick wires in the seam of my trousers.

Without speaking, they took the lantern, backed from the cell, and locked the door.

In the darkness, I groped across the floor until I found my locus magicalicus, which had stopped glowing, and put it into my pocket. Then I found my boots and put them on again.

I sat down with my back against the wall. I felt suddenly very tired. Nevery wasn't going to come and get me out, as he'd done before, when the duchess's guards had caught me in the Dawn Palace. Without lockpicks, I couldn't open the door.

A creeping dread seeped into me, along with the cold from the wall and the stone floor. *You will simply be left here*, Crowe had said. Left here to die, he meant, though that would take a while. Four or five days. I edged into the corner and curled up with my head on my knees, my arms wrapped around me.

The stone room was completely dark and silent. Hours passed. I grew colder and colder. Nevery would not come. The Underlord had left me here while he killed Wellmet's magic. There was nothing I could do about it. My shivering turned to shaking.

Something touched the top of my head. I looked up, clenching my teeth to hold the shivers in. Nothing, just silence. Then something soft and bitterly cold brushed along my cheek. I jerked away, my eyes wide, seeing nothing.

I reached into my pocket and pulled out my locus magicalicus. *'Lothfalas,'* I whispered. The light flashed, and died down to cast a thin glowing circle around me. In the glow I saw, hovering above me, right below the stone ceiling, a writhing mass of shadows. As I watched, a long, black shadow, rippling like a silken scarf, unravelled from the mass and probed down toward me. I scrambled away, but felt its radiating cold and dread.

Misery eels. A whole nest of them.

'Lothfalas,' I said again, louder. The light from my locus stone pulsed and then contracted. The mass of eels flinched away from the light, then spread across the ceiling. A few rippling shadows snaked down the walls; others gathered in the corners.

I clenched my locus magicalicus. The light dimmed. The eels writhed beyond the dim circle of light, waiting. The light dimmed. *'Lothfalas,'* I said, my voice sounding wavery and scared. A faint glow seeped from the stone. The eels pressed closer, closer.

Lothfalas. Lothfalas. Lothfalas.

According to gauge, magic level extremely low. Worried. Feel something is about to happen. Tried scrying globes again, still nothing. Did boy go to Crowe? Or is he up to something else?

After dark, Keeston came in. Pale, shaking with cold. Teeth chattering. —I saw him, Magister. I think it was him. Keeston paused, trembling. —It had to be him, sir. They had a bag over his head.

—What are you talking about? I asked.

—M-magister Nevery, my master sent me to work for you so I could report to him everything that happened here. I didn't want to do it, sir, but I had to. I'm very s-sorry.

—So you are a spy, too? I asked. Getting angry. Keeston looked confused. —Too, sir?

—My apprentice has been reporting to the Underlord, I said.

Keeston dried tears. —Conn? No, sir, he would never spy on you.

—You are mistaken, I said. —He is with Crowe at this very moment.

Keeston shook his head. —No he isn't, sir. Or if he is, he doesn't want to be. That's what I came here to tell you. Pettivox's men captured Conn and locked him in a storeroom. The Underlord was coming; I think they're going to k-kill him.

Drat the boy. Benet is sure, and now Keeston. Want to believe them. Only one way to be certain.

CHAPTER 34

I was being stupid.

'Lothfalas,' I said again, and got to my feet. The light from my locus magicalicus grew even fainter, a glow that lit only my hand, making it look green and pale. The rest of the cell seethed with darkness. A misery eel dropped down from the ceiling and settled on the back of my neck, a cold, bitter weight. Shuddering, I

reached back and touched it with my locus stone and it dropped off, but another one oozed up from the floor and twined around my leg. Kicking it away, I lunged for the door. In the faint glow of my locus stone, I saw the lock, rusty, the dark keyhole in the centre.

I placed my locus magicalicus over the lock; with my other hand I pushed a misery eel away from my face. *'Sessamay!'* I shouted, and followed with every single gate opening spell I knew. *Open!* I told the lock. These were not the right spells; the magic might not understand what I was asking for. But if the magic wanted me to save it, it would have to help me get away from the eels, out of the cell.

Nothing happened. Not even a flicker or flare of magic. More eels dropped down from overhead, a dead, cold weight; others rippled from the floor, up my legs. An icy scarf flowed around my neck, tightened. I caught my breath, slammed the stone against the lock, and gasped out the opening spells again.

The glow from the locus stone flicked out; the misery eels tangled around me. Then the magic gathered itself. The locus stone spat out a burst of sizzling sparks, which shot into the lock and exploded. I threw myself against the door, turning the knob, and, trailing misery eels, fell out of the cell into the hallway.

Nevery was there. The door opening knocked him backward onto the floor; lockpick wires and his cane went flying. He'd been trying to pick the lock to get me out.

Keeston stood beside him, eyes wide, clutching a lantern. I landed on the floor, eels swarming over me.

'Curse it, boy,' Nevery said. 'What are you doing?'

'Watch out for the eels!' I shouted. Reacting to the lantern light, the misery eels covering me oozed away. A shadowy mass of them gathered in the cell doorway.

Nevery saw them. He snatched up his cane and got to his feet. 'The light should hold them,' he said. 'Are you all right, boy?'

'Yes, fine,' I said, my voice shaking. I scrambled away from the door. An eel reached out into the corridor, testing. Keeston flinched.

'Don't drop the light, Keeston,' Nevery growled.

We'd be dead if he did.

Nevery straightened and scowled at me. 'Why didn't you answer when I called?'

From outside the door? 'I didn't hear you,' I said. The eels must have muffled the sound.

'Hmph,' Nevery said. 'Well, come along.' He whirled and went *tap tap tap*ping down the hallway, Keeston and I following. The lantern light made a bubble of safety around us, and we left the misery eels behind.

We went up the stairs to the ground floor of Pettivox's house, which I hadn't seen before because I'd had a bag over my head. It was dark and echoing and empty.

Keeston went ahead of us with the lantern. Nevery dropped back to walk beside me. 'Well?' He frowned down at me.

'Nevery, I'm not Crowe's,' I said.

'I have realized that, boy.'

'Here's the front door,' Keeston said over his shoulder.

Benet was there, standing guard over two of

Pettivox's men, both gagged and tied up with ropes. Benet nodded when he saw me. 'Found him?'

'Yes,' Nevery said, pausing to button up his cloak. 'Take him and Keeston back to Heartsease.' He headed for the door.

'No, Nevery,' I said.

He stopped and looked back at me. 'Come along, boy,' he said impatiently. 'You've caused enough trouble and confusion already. The magic level has fallen drastically during the past two days; I have a meeting to attend at Magisters Hall.'

I shook my head.

'What, boy?' Nevery said. Benet stepped closer to hear, and Keeston stood beside us with the lantern.

I clenched my hands. He wasn't going to believe me. 'The Underlord and Pettivox are stealing the magic tonight, Nevery. Right now. We have to stop them.'

'Boy,' Nevery began. 'I do not—'

'Nevery,' I interrupted, getting desperate. 'I went to Dusk House today. Last night, I mean. I saw the machine.' I shivered, remembering its pulsing and crashing and the empty hole it had left in the night when it had sucked in the magic. 'The Underlord and Pettivox built a prisoning device. A capacitor. They've captured almost all the city's magic. If we don't go now and stop them, they will steal it all and Wellmet will die.'

'You claim you saw a machine?' Nevery asked. 'Some kind of device?'

I nodded. 'It was huge.'

'In the Underlord's mansion? How did you get inside?'

I opened my mouth to answer.

'Never mind,' Nevery said quickly. 'I don't want to know.' He stared down at me, pulling on the end of his beard.

'I'll go by myself if I have to, Nevery,' I said.

'You would go and do what, boy? Stop the Underlord? Destroy this magical device?'

I nodded. The magic had chosen me for this; I wasn't going to let it die without trying to help it.

For a moment, all was still. I held my breath, waiting. Nevery could decide I was a liar and a thief, or he could trust me.

'Hmmm,' Nevery said. 'A prisoning device. I suppose such a thing is possible.' He looked down at me. 'All this time, boy, and you've never lied to me?'

I shook my head. I never had.

Slowly, Nevery nodded. 'Well then. We will go together.'

CHAPTER 35

When we stepped out of Pettivox's house, it was night again. I'd spent the whole day in the basement room.

'We need to warn the duchess and ask her to

send guards to Dusk House,' I said.

Nevery paused at the bottom of the steps. 'Benet can go.'

'Keeston would be better,' I said. He was all right, and we needed Benet with us.

Nevery raised his eyebrows. 'Would he?' He looked over at Keeston. 'Well, Keeston. Can you be trusted?'

Keeston, still gripping the lantern, gulped, then nodded. 'Yes, sir. I swear it. You can trust me, I promise, and—'

'Yes, all right,' Nevery interrupted. 'Run to the Dawn Palace and tell the duchess what is happening. Tell her we've gone ahead to the Twilight, and that she must send as many guardsmen as she can. Understand?'

'Yes, sir,' Keeston said. He spun and raced off, slipping a bit on the snow.

'Let's go,' I said, and Nevery, Benet, and I headed toward the Night Bridge, to cross into the Twilight.

The streets were deserted and dark; the werelights had gone out. The night felt desolate, empty. I put my hand in my pocket to check on my locus magicalicus, and it felt empty, too, and dead. The magic was gone.

We rushed down the hill like three black shadows, our feet crunching on the icy street, until we reached the Night Bridge. Ahead, the road led into the narrow way between the buildings on the bridge.

'Hold up,' Benet said suddenly, and grabbed Nevery and me by the arms to stop us. We stood, our breath steaming on the frigid air. Ahead, the bridge was completely dark, like a cave.

'What's the matter?' Nevery asked.

Benet shook his head. 'Too quiet. Underlord might've posted guards.'

'Benet, we can't wait,' I whispered.

Benet pulled a truncheon out of his belt. 'Follow.'

He led the way onto the dark bridge. Our footsteps sounded very loud in the silence.

Then, from out of the shadows, five dark shapes emerged. Minions. They didn't stop to warn us off, they just leaped at us, wielding clubs.

Benet stepped up to meet them, truncheon swinging. 'Go!' he shouted over his shoulder. He ducked a punch.

Nevery and I backed up, our way across the bridge blocked. Three of the minions followed, until Benet threw his truncheon. It whirled through the air and clipped a minion on the back of the head; he fell over like a chopped tree. Benet leaped on the others. 'I'll deal with these,' he shouted. 'Just go!'

We turned and hurried away. I turned and looked over my shoulder and saw one of the minions wrench himself from Benet's grip and start after us. We went faster.

We didn't speak; the minion following us didn't shout. I heard my own panting breaths, and Nevery's, and the tap of Nevery's cane, and the *crunch crunch crunch* of our feet and the pursuing feet on the icy road.

We put on a burst of speed and rounded a corner, Nevery's cloak flaring as he spun around. He pulled out his locus magicalicus. *'Remirrimer,'* he said, and started muttering a spell.

Not enough magic. The minion was getting closer. I pulled on his sleeve. 'Come on!'

Nevery cursed, and we started off again. 'This way,' I said, and pointed down a street that led toward the river.

In the Sunrise, the riverbanks were walls built of stone, with stone stairways leading down to wooden docks. We paused on the riverbank, catching our breaths.

The air was absolutely still and brittle cold; if somebody hit it, it would shatter into a thousand sharp-edged pieces. There was no sound of rushing water.

I pointed at the river. 'It's frozen. I think we can cross on the ice.'

'Yes,' Nevery said, straightening, and then the minion was on us. He was big and brawny; he shoved me out of the way and swung a fist at Nevery.

Nevery grappled with him and they went rolling down the nearest set of stone stairs, down to a dock. I raced down after them, leaped from the bottom step onto the minion's back, and bit him on the ear. It tasted worse than the rat's tail. The minion shook me off; then Nevery swung the gold knob of his cane into the minion's face.

'Hah!' he shouted.

The minion staggered back, blood streaming from his nose.

I scrambled to my feet. 'You all right?' I asked.

'Yes, boy,' Nevery gasped. Behind us, the minion put his hands to his face and shook his head. Drops of blood spattered around him.

I turned to survey the river. It was laid out before us, still, frozen, the ice clean and smoothly black. To the left loomed the Night Bridge; no lights shone from the opposite shore.

Carefully, I stepped out onto the ice. Without speaking, Nevery followed.

We set off, sliding our feet along, *skff skff*, Nevery using his cane to balance himself. The riverbank receded behind us. Overhead, the sky was black and stars shone down as bright as daggers.

Halfway across, we paused. My breath puffed out in white clouds before my face. I looked back across the ice. The minion was coming.

'Keep going,' Nevery said.

Under my feet, the ice trembled. 'Wait,' I

whispered. I bent down and put my hand flat on the surface. The cold burned. And I felt the river rushing by, just below my fingers.

Slowly, I stood up. The ice creaked. It was thin, barely covering the water. 'We'll have to go around,' I whispered.

Nevery nodded, and we edged around the thin ice, and then headed for the dark Twilight bank again.

I looked back over my shoulder. The minion, a dark shape against the dark ice, thought he could catch us by going the short way across – he reached the thin ice and went on. 'He's going to fall in,' I said.

As I spoke, the ice beneath the minion gave way and, like a stone dropping into a puddle, he plunged into the river, cursing and thrashing. I glanced at Nevery.

'Keep going,' he said grimly.

We kept going, expecting the ice to crack under our feet and send us into the freezing water, too.

As we neared the Twilight bank, I saw that the tenements and warehouses were all dark and still. At the very edge of the river, we climbed the rocky bank and up onto a rutted path that led along the side of a warehouse.

We paused for a moment, catching our breaths, then I started off again.

'Wait, boy,' Nevery said.

'We can't wait, Nevery,' I said. 'It might be too late already.' I started walking, fast, and Nevery strode along beside me. We came around the corner of the warehouse and headed up the nearest steep street, which was edged with tumbledown tenement houses.

'Too late for what, exactly?' Nevery asked.

I shook my head. I hadn't really had time to think it all through. 'The Underlord built the device to capture all the magic.'

'If that is what the device is for,' Nevery said, 'it would appear that he plans to hold the city hostage.'

Right. Magic wasn't just for running the factories or keeping the werelights lit, it was the lifeblood of the city. With the device, Crowe's calculations told him, he would control all the magic, and the people would have to pay him for it. He would rule the city, all of it, not just the Twilight. But the Underlord was wrong. 'Nevery, the magic can't stay inside that prison device. It will die.' And soon, if we didn't let it out.

'Boy, the magic isn't alive.'

I wasn't going to argue with him about it. But if we didn't hurry, it would be too late.

We climbed the streets until we reached Dusk House. We peered in through the barred gate. The building was still, dark and silent, but the air felt wound tight. Waiting.

'We ought to wait for the duchess's guards,' Nevery said softly.

I shook my head. The guards would have to fight through the minions on the Night Bridge, and that might take too long.

'I don't suppose you have a plan,' Nevery said.

No, I didn't. 'I think we just have to go in, Nevery,' I said.

'This is why you get into trouble, boy,' Nevery muttered.

'Come on,' I said.

Staying in the shadows, I led Nevery through the gate and around to the back of the Underlord's mansion, to the door I'd gone in when disguised as a cat. It was unguarded.

We made our way through the dark hallways, stopping now and then to listen, hearing nothing. The minions were all off blocking the bridge, I realized. They hadn't expected anyone to cross the ice. Sure as sure, though, they hadn't left the device completely unguarded.

Finally we came to the room with the entrance to the underground workshop. The bookcase-door was closed, the room dark.

'The bookcase opens,' I whispered to Nevery. I led him across the room, then reached up to push the panel that opened it. The bookcase swung open and the stairway gaped like a pit before us.

Without hesitating, I led Nevery down the narrow stairway to the second turning, and peered around. The lights in the cavernous workroom were dimmed; in the centre of the shadowy room squatted the prisoning device, swollen and shiny, like a giant leech well fed on blood. Its gears and pistons were still, and the slowsilver was frozen in its crystal tubes. The riveted storage tank in the middle bulged. The magic was caught in there. Down in my bones, I felt a squealing hum, the magic straining at the prison, trying to escape. I also felt a faint tingle in the air; a very little bit of the magic was left, lingering outside the device where the rest of it was trapped.

Down in the pit, a few minions were lounging around in the shadows, and, by one of the chart-covered tables, Pettivox sat writing something by the light of his locus stone.

I put my hand into my pocket to check on my own locus magicalicus. A stone could be destroyed by magic, Nevery had told me once, and its wizard with it. I took a deep breath. The magic had chosen me for this, I reminded myself. I couldn't go off and let it die. I marked out a path from the stairs to the device. I had to try, at least.

I eased around the corner.

'What are you doing, boy?' I heard Nevery

whisper, but I kept going, creeping down the stairs.

One of the minions shouted, his voice echoing in the huge workroom. At the sound, Pettivox glanced up from the table. Seeing me, he stood bolt upright, his chair crashing to the floor behind him. *'You!'* he shouted. I got to the bottom of the stairs and started to run.

The minions closed in; I kept going, across the stone floor, toward the device. I wasn't sure what I was going to do when I got there. If I got there.

A minion made a grab at me; another one caught at my sleeve, but I eeled away. Pettivox strode across the room, shouting, his words lost in the echoes. I whirled away from another minion, and Pettivox was there, seizing me by the hair, lifting me off my feet. Two minions grabbed me. I twisted and wriggled like a worm on a fishhook, but they had me.

Pettivox let me go, drew his hand back, and struck me a crashing blow across the face; if the minions hadn't been holding me I would have fallen. 'You,' he snarled again.

I shook my head. One of my teeth was loose and I had blood in my mouth. Black spots danced before my eyes. From where I stood, the minions gripping my arms tightly, I saw the device looming overhead, the dim light glinting off its gears and wires.

Pettivox leaned over me, teeth bared. 'You're dead, thief. The Underlord will return shortly, and he will kill you himself.' He drew back his fist to hit me again. I closed my eyes and clenched my teeth.

But then came a shout. 'Pettivox!' Nevery bellowed. My eyes popped open.

Down the stairs Nevery strode, his grey cloak swirling. At the bottom, he swung his knob-headed cane and slammed it into a table cluttered with leftover copper parts; they clattered to the ground.

Pettivox jerked up and around.

The minions holding me stared, but their grips didn't loosen.

Striding across the floor, drawing on the magic left outside the device, Nevery began a spell, a river of words that flowed from his mouth and swelled to fill the room, echoing from the walls. Just beneath the ceiling, way overhead, wisps of fog appeared, then gathered into clouds, grey and plump with rain. The giant workroom grew dark.

Nevery shouted the last word of the spell and the clouds rumble-rolled together. Lightning flashed down. With a shriek, Pettivox leaped out of the way, and the bolt scorched the ground where he'd stood. The minions holding me staggered back. Thunder growled.

Nevery started another spell; Pettivox was shouting a spell of his own. Their voices echoed from the walls.

Overhead, the clouds' bellies swelled, then exploded. Bolts of lightning zinged in all directions, ricocheting from one stone wall to the other, and then crashing into the device. Sparks leaped from its rivets and gears, but the magic stayed locked within.

A sizzling blue bolt whizzed just over my head. The two minions holding me flinched. That was all I needed.

With a twist of my shoulders, I pulled myself

out of the minions' hands, kicked one of them in the shins, and sprinted toward the device. The minions shouted and followed, right on my heels.

Reaching the device, I scrambled up the stone base it rested on, then climbed onto a piston. The metal sparked under my fingers. One of the minions, coming after me, jumped for my foot, but I reached up to a gear and pulled myself out of his reach. I climbed higher, over tubes, clinging to hoses, until I reached the bulging storage tank.

Out in the workroom, Nevery and Pettivox were shouting at each other, their voices echoing off the stone walls. Thunder crashed again and the clouds opened, releasing a torrent of freezing rain.

Blinking water from my eyes, I climbed higher. The rain hit the device and turned to ice; I hung on with numb fingers. A minion climbed up from below me. Another one shouted and threw a bottle; it shattered just over my head, and I shut my eyes as shards of glass rained down.

Opening my eyes, I pulled my locus magicalicus from my coat pocket. The jewel glowed in the stormy light.

I didn't know any spells for this. I rested my forehead against the freezing copper skin of the storage tank and gently tapped my locus stone against the tank. It made a tinny chiming sound.

Come out, I told the magic. *Just come through the stone.*

Inside its prison, the magic strained; I felt it, confined, desperate, dying.

Another bottle shattered beside my head. The minion climbing up from below grabbed my ankle and pulled. I slipped and almost dropped my locus stone, then gripped an icy cogwheel with my other hand and held on. The minion pulled harder; I kicked him, and then I kicked him again. Screaming, the minion fell away, bouncing off the side of the device before crashing to the floor.

I pulled myself back up to the storage tank. With shaking hands, I moved my locus magicalicus over the surface of the tank and held it against one of the riveted seams. 'Come out,' I whispered. 'Here's a good place.' Again I tapped my locus stone against the seam. The magic strained against the tank. The riveted seam creaked and bulged, but held.

'Here, magic,' I whispered again. Within the tank, the magic stilled, shifted, and focused itself on my locus magicalicus, on me. It was like looking up at a night sky full of stars and having the stars suddenly look back.

I closed my eyes. *Calm breath, still hands.* I thought my way through my locus stone and into the device, and opened the lock. *Here. Come out.*

The room held its breath. I heard no shouting, no thunder or wind, no sizzling bolts of lightning. Just a black and velvety silence that filled my head and stilled my breath.

The riveted seam along the side of the tank bulged, then, like cloth ripping, split. With the crash of thunder and lightning striking at the same time, the magic burst from the device and through my locus stone, roaring through me. It filled my sight, a wave of flashing, crashing light, sparks, blazing white flames, a thousand stars. I clung to my locus magicalicus, and the magic kept coming, pouring out until it filled the workroom, then exploding upwards, blowing the top off the device, smashing through Dusk House, fountaining out into the dark night. In my hand, my locus magicalicus disintegrated into a puff of sparkling dust. I was flung away like a leaf in the wind.

I expected to be dead.

But instead everything went still. Inside my head, the magic said something, its words a deep, rumbling hum inside my skull and down in the heavier bones of my arms and legs. I floated, wrapped in a warm and welcoming blanket of light.

And then everything went dark.

Device destroyed now, and we can hope to never see its like again in this world. Destroyed, at cost of boy's locus magicalicus, possibly his life.

After boy released the confined magic and Dusk House was razed, found myself at the bottom of gaping pit in darkness, a few small fires burning, debris everywhere, dust sifting down, rubble settling. Not a trace of the device; it had been utterly destroyed.

Managed to kindle bit of light with lothfalas spell and searched ruins for the boy. Found him wedged in a narrow crack that had opened in one stone wall, as if he'd been set there for safekeeping. Way in blocked by debris. Thought boy was dead. Pale, cold, unmoving. Covered with fine, scintillant dust — the remains of his locus magicalicus. A loss too great to bear.

Duchess's guards arrived then, and Benet, who helped me pull the beams and rubble away from boy's body. Had him out, finally. Placed my hand on his chest, found he was still breathing.

Wrapped him in my robe and Benet's coat, took him

home to Heartsease, put him to bed.

Had Trammel in to look at him. Not a mark on the boy, Trammel said. No apparent injury. He is simply cold and exhausted. Needs to sleep. Keep him warm and wait for him to wake up.

So now we wait.

CHAPTER 36

I woke up. Even with my eyes closed, I knew where I was; I recognized the musty-dusty smell of my attic room. But I was lying in a bed covered with blankets, and the room was warm.

My locus magicalicus was gone. I had a hollow, dark, echoing place inside me where it had been. But the magic was safe, at least. I felt it in the air, all around me, even warmer than the blankets.

I opened my eyes. Yes, my room. I was in a bed, and a fire burned in the hearth. Bright sunlight shone in through the windows and lay across the floor, shining on my dragon painting. In a chair beside the bed sat Nevery, his head tilted back, asleep.

Carefully, I sat up, my back to the wall beside my bed. That was enough; the room spun around me and I felt like I might fall over.

My movement woke Nevery. He tipped his head down, blinking, and rubbed the back of his neck. Then he looked over at me. His eyes widened. 'Well, boy?' he said. His voice sounded rusty.

I nodded. The room wavered, and I closed my eyes. I felt Nevery's hand under my chin. I opened my eyes again. Nevery frowned down at me. 'I'm all right,' I said.

He looked me over, then let me go and sat back down in his chair. 'Do you remember what happened?'

Talking was better than nodding. 'Yes,' I said. Actually, no. 'What happened to Pettivox? And to Underlord Crowe?'

'Hmmm. You should have told me from the start that Crowe is your uncle.'

Yes, I should have. But I didn't want to talk about it.

Nevery waited for a moment, then went on. 'Pettivox disappeared after the device was destroyed and is presumed dead. Crowe is in the duchess's prison cells, awaiting her justice.'

Oh. I wondered if she'd send him to the gallows tree. I doubted it. She preferred to exile people. I felt suddenly very tired.

'Benet is well,' Nevery went on. 'And Keeston.' He said something more, but my eyes closed and I started falling sideways. Nevery stopped talking and caught me, and gently eased me down.

The ladder up to my room creaked and I heard Benet's deep voice.

'No, he's asleep,' Nevery said.

And then I was.

When I woke up again, the room was dark except for a dying fire in the hearth, and Keeston was the one asleep in the chair beside my bed.

And I felt a little better.

I sat up and the room didn't spin. My lost locus magicalicus was still an empty, aching space inside me. But I didn't want to think about it. I was thirsty. In the shadows across the room was a small table with Benet's knitting on it, along with a few teacups and a jug, which might have water in it. I swung my legs out of bed and stood up. A mistake. The room started swirling around, and then I found myself getting a close-up look at the floor.

Keeston sat up with a jerk, and I heard someone climbing up the ladder. The trapdoor opened and Benet bulled his way in, holding a candle.

'I'm all right,' I said. 'I just fell over.'

Benet set the candle on the table, then stomped over, picked me up, and put me back into bed, ducking his head to keep it from bumping the sloped ceiling. Then he glared at Keeston. 'You were told to watch him.'

Blinking, Keeston gripped his locus magicalicus. 'S-sorry,' he said.

Benet swung around to glare at me. 'You

hungry?'

Yes, I was. Ravenous.

'Stay in bed,' Benet ordered. He pointed at Keeston. 'Watch him.' Then he went down the ladder.

I sat up and leaned against the wall.

'You're supposed to stay in bed,' Keeston said, nervous.

'I am in bed,' I said.

'No,' Keeston said. 'You should be lying down.'

I shrugged. 'I feel better sitting up.' Which wasn't exactly true, but I'd need to sit up anyway when Benet brought food. I looked Keeston over; he seemed tired and twitchy. 'Are you all right?' I asked.

He flinched. He was still clutching his locus magicalicus. Right. I knew what he was afraid of. His master's master was in the duchess's prison; maybe he thought he would be arrested, too. 'Don't worry,' I said. 'Nevery will tell everyone that you helped us. And he knows you didn't know what Pettivox was up to.'

Keeston stared at me. 'But I did know.'

'Not everything,' I said. 'You didn't know about that device.'

He relaxed just a little. 'No, I didn't.' We sat in silence for a few minutes. The candle flame flickered, sending dark shadows wavering over the walls. Then he asked, in a rush, 'Do you think Magister Nevery would let me come and be his apprentice?'

The question dropped into the hole inside me that my locus stone had left and echoed around. I wasn't a wizard anymore; without a locus magicalicus, I wasn't even an apprentice. I swallowed down a lump of unhappiness. 'I don't know,' I managed to say. 'Nevery didn't like having me as an apprentice.'

'Yes he does,' Keeston said. 'Will you ask him for me?'

'You should ask him yourself,' I said. He might even say yes.

At that moment, Benet climbed into the room, carrying a tray, which he set down on the table after pushing aside the teacups and jug. He'd brought another candle, too, so the room was brighter.

He gave me a biscuit and a cup of tea and I ate them, but they didn't fill up the hole inside.

After a few days, I was well enough to look after myself. Late in the morning, I got out of bed and put on my clothes, and, carrying my boots, made my way downstairs to the kitchen. Benet was there, cutting up apples.

'You're up,' he said.

I nodded. Lady uncurled herself from the hearthstone and padded over to me, purring. I set down my boots and sat beside the fire so she could climb into my lap.

'You going to put those on?' Benet said. I looked up. He was pointing at my boots.

'They're too small for my feet,' I said. The black sweater fitted better, too; I must have grown while I was in bed.

'You'll have to have new ones,' Benet said. He set aside his bowl of apple slices and started rolling out pastry.

So Benet thought I would be staying at Heartsease. I wasn't so sure Nevery would agree. Without a locus stone, I couldn't be his apprentice anymore, and he knew I wouldn't be a servant. And I wasn't a thief or a lockpick; I couldn't go back to living on the streets of the Twilight.

'Master Nevery said if you were up today, you should find him at the academicos library.'

But I wouldn't be able to get through the tunnel gates to reach the academicos. Drats.

'He left a keystone for you.' Benet pointed with a floury finger at my coat, which hung from a nail beside the door. The stone was in the pocket, I guessed.

'Thanks,' I said. I pushed Lady off my lap and got to my feet and, after putting on my coat, went down the stairs and outside. The sun shone brightly and the air smelled fresh, though it was still chilly. All the snow had melted. The big tree across the courtyard was empty of birds, but the twigs at the ends of its black branches were tipped with red, swelling buds. Winter was over, at last.

Which was a good thing. I wasn't used to being barefoot. Crossing the courtyard, the cobbles felt cold and wet under my feet.

I walked slowly through the tunnels, using the keystone to get through the gates. The magic leaped from the stone to the locks, fresh and sparkling. The magical being was feeling better, I figured.

Before climbing the stairs to the academicos, I had to rest, leaning against the tunnel wall. I got to the top of the stairs and stopped to catch my breath. Across the courtyard, grey-robed students were standing in groups, talking and playing games, basking in the end-of-winter sunshine. Rowan left a group and came over to me; she was wearing her grey student's robe and carrying her book bag.

She gave me a hug. She was only a little taller than I was, I realized; I really had grown. I rested my head on her shoulder for a moment.

She stepped back and looked me over. 'I see you've decided not to wear your shoes, Connwaer.'

'My feet are too big for them,' I said.

'Mmm-hmmm,' she said. 'My mother would like you to come and see her.'

All right. But now I had to find Nevery in the

library.

We turned to walk across the courtyard to the academicos. As Rowan and I passed, the students stopped what they were doing and stared. I put my head down and kept walking; Rowan raised her chin and looked proud and sharp, like the first day I'd met her.

We went up the stairs and inside.

Brumbee was standing before his office, speaking with Periwinkle. When he saw us, he left her and came over.

'My dear Conn,' he said, smiling. 'So glad to see you're feeling better. We were all quite worried.' He looked down at my feet. 'I see you're not wearing any shoes . . . ?'

'My boots are too small,' I said.

'Ah. Well, I'm sure Nevery will see to it. Now, as soon as you're well enough, we expect to see you back in your classes again.'

He did?

'I have class now,' Rowan said. 'I'll have somebody row me to Heartsease later to help you catch up on what you missed, all right?'

'Thanks,' I said. Rowan smiled, hefted her

book bag over her shoulder, and left.

Brumbee beamed. 'Good! Now, Nevery is up in the library, if you're looking for him.'

As I climbed the stairs to the library, the academicos students started streaming in from the courtyard for their first class, chattering, filling the gallery with noise.

I opened the door to the library, went inside, and closed it. Nevery was at a table near the window. At the sound of the door closing, he looked up and nodded.

I waited by the door while he gathered up his knob-headed cane and a canvas book bag, buttoned up his robe, put on his hat, and came across to meet me.

We stepped out into the hallway. A few students edged past where we stood, shooting us curious, sideways glances.

Nevery leaned on his cane and frowned down at me. 'Well, come along,' he said. He turned and started down the stairs, step step *tap*, step step *tap*.

I followed, but didn't say anything.

We came to the front entry of the academicos

and went out and down the steps to the wide courtyard. All the students had gone in.

Nevery dropped the book bag at his feet and cleared his throat. 'You look like you should still be in bed.'

I wrapped my arms around myself. Even though the sun was warm, the breeze from the river was chilly. 'I'm all right, Nevery,' I said.

'So you keep saying, boy. But I don't think you are.'

I looked down at my bare toes.

Nevery sighed. 'You lost your locus magicalicus.'

I nodded.

'And your boots, apparently.'

'I've grown out of them,' I said.

'Yes, I expect you have,' he said. With his cane, he poked the bag at his feet. 'Look in there.'

I went down on my knees and rummaged in the bag. 'This?' I held up a book.

'No,' Nevery said. The breeze gusted, and he clapped his hand to his head to keep his hat from blowing away. 'The robe.'

Every wizard and apprentice wore a robe; all

the students at the academicos had one, too, like Rowan, grey with a patch on the sleeve which indicated their family or house. In the bag, among the books, a wax-stoppered bottle, and a few stray papers, was a robe. I pulled it out, stood, and handed it to Nevery.

He handed it back to me. 'It's for you, boy,' he said. 'You're a student and an apprentice. You need a robe.'

Oh. I took off my coat and slipped the robe on over my sweater. Its grey wool was moth-eaten and spattered with scorch marks, and the ragged hem brushed the ground. On one sleeve was a patch, embroidered in faded blue thread with the same hourglass with wings symbol that was etched into the stone before the Heartsease tunnel gate and stamped in gold on the front cover of Nevery's chronicle of locus stones.

Nevery leaned over and touched the patch. 'The winged hourglass. My family's crest.'

The robe had been his when he was a student.

Carefully, I buttoned the front of the robe and rolled up the sleeves, which hung down over my hands.

'One thing I'm sure as sure about, Conn,' Nevery said, his voice gruff. 'You are a wizard, and you will find another locus magicalicus.'

I took a deep breath. Yes. Yes, Nevery was right.

I was a wizard. I would study at the academicos and learn every spell I could, and I would try to convince the magisters that the magic was a living being. And one day, if I didn't find a locus magicalicus in Wellmet, I would go out into the world to search for it.

'Well, my boy,' Nevery said. 'Let's go home.' He set off across the empty courtyard, and after a moment I followed.

I ran to catch up. 'Nevery,' I said, 'I think I'm going to need a room to work in.'

He strode on. 'A workroom, boy?'

I nodded. I had a lot of work to do. I didn't have a locus magicalicus, so I'd have to figure out a way to get the magic's attention so I could talk to it and it could talk back to me. 'I'm going to need slowsilver, too. And tourmalifine.'

Nevery paused at the top of the stairs leading down to the tunnel and shot me one of his keen-gleam looks. 'But when tourmalifine and slow-silver mingle, boy, they explode.'

I grinned. Yes, Nevery, I know.

A GUIDE TO
WELLMET'S
PEOPLE AND
PLACES

PEOPLE

BENET – A rather scary-looking guy, but one who loves to knit, bake and clean. His nose has been broken so many times, it's been flattened. If he were an animal he'd be a big bear. His hair is brown and sticks out on his head like spikes. You wouldn't want to meet him in a dark alley, but you would want to eat his biscuits.

CONN – Has shaggy black hair that hangs down over his bright blue eyes. He's been a gutterboy for most of his life, so he's watchful and a little wary; at the same time, he's completely pragmatic and truthful. He's thin, but he's sturdy and strong, too. He has a quirky smile (hence the cat's quirked tail). Conn does not know his own age; it could be anywhere from twelve to fourteen. A great friend to have, but be careful that you don't have anything valuable in your pockets in reach of his sticky fingers.

 **NEVERY FLINGLAS** – Is tall with grey hair, a long grey beard, shaggy grey eyebrows and sharp, keen black eyes. He's impatient and grumpy and often hasty, but beneath that his heart is kind (he would never admit it). Mysterious and possibly dangerous, Nevery is a difficult wizard to read, but a good one to know.

 **PETTIVOX** – Very tall and broad, with white hair and beard, very white teeth and red lips. He's the master to Keeston. Conn dislikes them both.

 **ROWAN FORESTAL** – A tall, slender girl of around fifteen, with short red hair and grey eyes. She is very intelligent with a good, if dry, sense of humour. She is the daughter of the

Duchess. She is also very interested in studying swordcraft.

THE DUCHESS – Willa Forestal is Rowan's mother and they are physically similar. She is a woman who bears a lot of responsibility, and it shows. She is highly intelligent but doesn't have a sense of humour, as Rowan does. The Duchess controls the Sunrise area of Wellmet, and she dislikes magic (though she realizes its necessity to the survival of Wellmet).

PLACES

ACADEMICOS – Set on an island in the river that runs between the Twilight and the Sunrise, the Acadmicos is a school for the rich students and potential wizards of Wellmet. Conn enrols there after becoming Nevery's apprentice.

DAWN PALACE – The home of the Duchess and Rowan. The palace itself is a huge, rectangular building – not very architecturally interesting, but with lots of decorations crusted on it to make it fancy.

DUSK HOUSE – The home to Underlord Crowe. This fortress like building is oppressive with narrow windows and a massive underground laby-rinth. Dusk House is guarded by hulking minions. To enter without an invitation is a death warrant.

HEARTSEASE – Nevery's ancestral island home. The middle of the house was blown up by Nevery's pyrotechnic experiments twenty years before this story. So the two ends of the house are left standing and the middle looks like it has a bite taken out.

MAGISTERS HALL – Seat of power for the wizards who control and guard the magic of Wellmet. It is a big, imposing grey stone building on an island with a wall built all the way around it at the waterline.

WELLMET RUNIC ALPHABET

In Wellmet, some people write using runes to stand for the letters of the alphabet. In fact, you may find some messages written in runes in THE MAGIC THIEF.

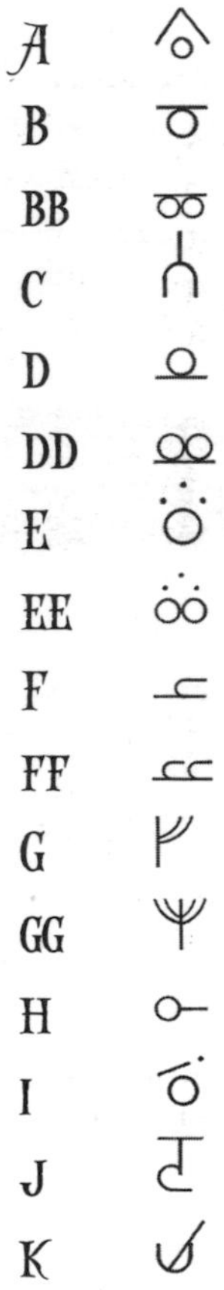

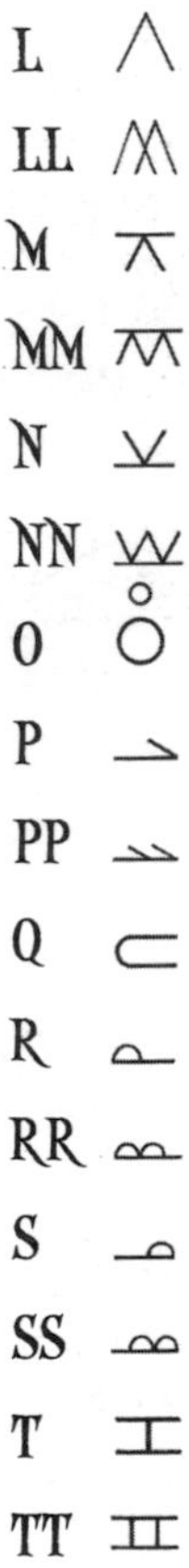

A	⌂	L	⋀	U	8
B	⊽	LL	⋀⋀	V	/
BB	⊽⊽	M	⊼	W	⊽
C	⌐	MM	⊼⊼	X	∅
D	�барат	N	⋁	Y	8
DD	∞	NN	⋁⋁	Z	✕
E	⊙	O	○		
EE	∴∴	P	⌐		
F	⊏	PP	⌐		
FF	⊏⊏	Q	⊂		
G	Ⱬ	R	⌐		
GG	Ψ	RR	⌐⌐		
H	⊙	S	⌐		
I	⊙	SS	⊂⊂		
J	⊐	T	⊢		
K	⅄	TT	⊬		

Uppercase letters are made by adding an extra line under a letter; for instance:

Uppercase A ⌂

Uppercase B ⊽

Runic punctuation: v

Beginning of a sentence: •

End of a sentence (period): :

Comma: ∼

Question mark: ⌐

BENET'S BISCUITS

300g all-purpose flour
1/2 teaspoon salt
4 teaspoons bee's wing (baking powder)
2 teaspoons sugar
110g butter
150ml milk

Preheat oven to 450°F. Mix dry ingredients together in bowl. Cut in butter until fine and crumbly. Make a well in these ingredients and pour in milk. Knead with your fingers only until blended — do not overwork or biscuits will be hard and flat. Roll to one knuckle thick and cut in rounds. Place on greased pan, and bake until golden brown (12 to 15 minutes). Best eaten hot, with butter and honey.

CONN'S BISCUITS

Put in bowl:
Some flour
A bit of water
Baking powder
A pinch of salt
A hunk of butter or lard

Mix up very well with wooden spoon. If it's watery, add more flour. Mix some more. Plop into pan, put pan in coals to bake for a while. Best eaten hot, with butter and honey.

THANKS TO...

Jenn Reese for her generous friendship and for believing in the power of story.

My agent, Caitlin Blasdell, and my editor, Melanie Donovan. And to the team at Harper-Collins: editorial assistant Greg Ferguson, editorial director Phoebe Yeh, copy editor Kathryn Silsand, designer Sasha Illingworth, artist Antonio Javier Caparo, and the goddesses of subrights, Camilla Borthwick, Jean McGinley, and Joan Rosen.

Sandra McDonald, Chance Morrison, Charlie Finlay, Toby Buckell, Dave Schwartz, Elizabeth Glover, Heather Shaw, Lisa Bradley, Deb Coates, Rachel Swirsky, Christopher East, Melissa Marr, Dean Lorey, Patrick Samphire, Tim Pratt, Paul Melko, and Steph Burgis (most especially), and a quadruple espresso thanks to Greg van Eekhout for hugely inspiring pep talks, for doodling on the manuscript, and for encouraging my bacon habit.

Anne and Ward Bing, and Anne Hankins. Warm and sunny thanks to Pat and Frank Hankins. And to my dear Theo and The Maud.

And most of all, thanks to John, best husband in the world. And yes, best critiquer, too.